STAR

G·K Hall &Cº.

Also by V.C. Andrews®
in Large Print:

Misty
Music in the Night
Raven
Runaways
Unfinished Symphony
Heart Song
Brooke
Butterfly
Crystal
Hidden Jewel
Pearl in the Mist
Midnight Whispers
Darkest Hour
Twilight's Child
Secrets of the Morning
Web of Dreams

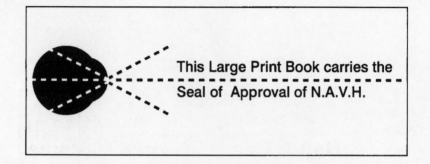

This Large Print Book carries the
Seal of Approval of N.A.V.H.

V.C. ANDREWS®

STAR

The Wildflowers #2

G.K. Hall & Co. • **Thorndike, Maine**

STAR

Prologue

When my grandmother drove me to Doctor Marlowe's for my second group therapy session, I sat in the car for a few moments and thought, girl, just have her turn around and take you home. What good is it going to do you to tell your troubles to these three rich white girls, although I did think Cathy, or Cat as Misty called her, wasn't as well-to-do as Misty and Jade seem to be.

As we drove into Doctor Marlowe's driveway, I saw Jade's chauffeured limousine pull away, so I knew I wasn't the first to arrive. I couldn't help wondering if Cat was coming back. The whole time Misty talked yesterday, Cathy the cat looked like she was sitting on a cold, wet park bench, ready to leap off and scoot into a dark alley the first chance she got. She sighed and squirmed and looked at the ceiling and the floor, everywhere but at us or at Doctor Marlowe. I think if she could have crawled under her seat, she would have.

My story wasn't at all like Misty's. It wasn't about spoiled rich boys and big houses with ballrooms and such. I wasn't going to complain about all the meaningless toys and dolls and clothes I was given. What I was given probably wouldn't fill a corner in one of their rooms anyway. And I wasn't going to describe parents who couldn't see eye to eye about their egos. The last thing my momma worried about was her makeup, her complexion, and whether or not her hair and clothes were in style. I couldn't even begin to imagine Daddy going to fancy gyms and wearing expensive sweat suits. If Cathy the cat thought Misty's descriptions of what she called a hard life were hard to swallow, she'd surely choke to death in Doctor Marlowe's office once I began telling about my life.

The thing is, did I want to begin? What were these girls going to tell me about me and my troubles that I didn't already know myself, huh? What did Doctor Marlowe expect out of us? I couldn't tell Misty anything that would help her yesterday. She wouldn't be able to tell me anything that would help me today. And that Jade . . . I was sure she'd be sitting there with her nose pointed at the ceiling, refusing to lower herself to look my way. I bet she'd make me feel like she was doing me a favor just staying in the room while I talked.

I had tossed and turned and fretted about it quite a while last night, worried they might laugh at me or think my story was beneath them. I didn't want to go in there and have to look at their smiles of ridicule.

Granny looked at me, surprised at my hesitation.

"What do you plan on doing, Star, just sitting there in the car all morning? You know I got chores to run."

"Coming here is a waste of time, Granny." I looked at her. "It is!"

"Yeah, well the doctors and the judge don't think so and that's what counts here, Star, so you just better get on in there. I can't abide any more trouble. Not with this old heart ticking down like some tired old grandfather clock," she said.

Granny knew that was all she had to say to get me to do what she wanted. There was nothing I feared more for myself and my brother Rodney than her having another heart attack. She was the only one left in the world who cared about us and loved us, and she was the only one we cared to love.

I opened the car door and started to slide out.

"Okay," she sang to the front window, "I guess there's no sugar for me this morning."

I shook my head and leaned over to give her a kiss on her plump right cheek. Then she grabbed my hand as I turned away and held it so tightly it sent a shiver down the bone and into my spine. Her face was like one of her pieces of antique china, full of tiny cracks, still beautiful, but on the verge of shattering the moment it was tapped a bit too hard.

Granny and I had the same eyes, only hers were just a bit rounder and somehow still lit up with hope more often than mine. However, this morning her eyes were full of worry, making them look heavy, so heavy she looked like she wanted to just close them and lay her head back on that double down pillow she claimed was full of good dreams.

How I wished I had a pillow like that.

Granny had had so many troubles in her life, troubles she had buried so deeply in her mountain of memories, I never even knew about them. She didn't want me to know. If I asked her too many questions about her own youth and her own hardships, she would just shake her head and say, "You don't need to feed the hatred living in your heart anything extra, Star. Your momma and daddy done enough to provide it with a feast that's kept it too fat as it is."

"What is it, Granny?" I asked as she squeezed my hand.

"You give Doctor Marlowe a chance to help you, Star. Don't shut up all the doors and windows, child, like you done so many times before. You're too young to become someone's lost cause, hear? Your momma likes to wear them shoes, but you kick 'em off."

"Yes, Granny," I said smiling.

If I had inherited just a small piece of that steel spine of hers, I would surely make it through all the rain and wind on the road ahead of me, I thought, and there was plenty still to come.

She let go and I continued out of the car.

"And don't look down on those other girls just because their families got some money," she warned me.

I shook my head at her.

"What do you know about people with money, Granny? You haven't ever had any rich friends to complain about, have you?"

"Never mind your smart mouth, child. I don't have to have rich friends to know having lots of money doesn't mean you don't need any sympathy and a helping hand. Those other girls wouldn't be here otherwise, would they?" she pointed out.

She was a smart one, my Granny. I guess something could be said for the school of hardship, too. Granny could be the valedictorian of that school and graduate with honors, I thought, not that it was something anyone would want or be proud of, especially Granny.

"Okay, Mrs. Anthony," I said. Whenever I called her by her name, she knew I was teasing her.

"You hold your tongue in there, child, and be civil, hear?" she warned me firmly.

"Yes, Granny."

"I'll be back the same time as yesterday," she said and started away.

I watched her drive off, a little old lady, not more than five feet four inches tall with shoulders still capable of holding up the responsibilities my much younger mother couldn't tolerate. Granny still had plenty of grit and walked proudly with her head high.

Granny always kept her smoke-gray hair brushed back and tied neatly in a bun. She wore just a touch of lipstick, but no other makeup, ever. Her eyeglasses were really the only frilly thing she permitted in her life. They were fashioned like expensive designer glasses with dark frames. It gave her just enough of a touch of style to make her comfortable with her public appearances, and she loved it when her older men friends kidded her and called her Miss America.

She was once a very pretty woman. She didn't look her sixty-eight years, despite the tensions and disappointments in her life. Granny wasn't as much of a churchgoer as most of her friends, but she had a deep faith in the goodness of people and the promise of an everlasting paradise at the end of the difficult journey. In her mind there were always people worse off, and she put more of her strength and energy into feeling sorrier for them than she did for herself. There was nothing she taught me that was more important to her than to despise and avoid self-pity. She said it was like "shackles around your ankles, keeping you chained to disaster and defeat. Instead, you pick yourself up when you get set back some and move on until it's time to stop and put your trust in the Lord," she advised.

Maybe you had to be old to believe like that, I thought. I wasn't ready to simply accept disappointments and defeat and move on. I refused to bend and I let whatever winds that blew at me know it. I'd break before I'd bend. Granny told me that was just defeating myself, but I still had the need to scratch and claw, kick and punch and spit into the faces of those who made my life miserable.

It was supposed to rain all day in Los Angeles and the clouds were blowing in from the northwest and thickening rapidly as the hands of the wind molded them like clay. Doctor Marlowe's large Tudor house looked darker, the windows reflecting the gray skies. It was a very big house, the biggest house I had ever been in, and here in one of the wealthiest neighborhoods in Brentwood, too.

There was nothing to reveal that Doctor Marlowe's house was a place where she treated patients, or clients, as they liked to call us. I guess that was deliberate. Doctor Marlowe certainly didn't want us to feel like freaks or anything. She wanted us all to be relaxed like people just visiting, but I had no other reason to come to this part of the city where so many rich people lived, no other reason than supposedly getting my head put back on straight.

However, no matter what the courts and the schools and the other doctors had said, I still didn't believe in the value of coming here even though Doctor Marlowe used words as her medicines. She prescribed different ways of thinking about things, used questions the way other doctors used X-rays and always tried to turn your eyes around so you were looking into yourself instead of at her.

I admit that she made me think about everything twice at least, but it still hadn't made me feel any better about myself or the things that had happened to me and my brother. I wasn't going to walk out of this big house and her office one day and be picked up by loving new parents, was I? She wasn't going to wave a magic wand over my horrible history and make it dissolve into thin air like some bad dream. I'd still be what Misty called an orphan with parents.

It was a good description. My mommy and daddy weren't dead and buried, but they were dead to me even though there were no funerals. Instead of a procession to the cemetery, there had been a parade of lies and crippled promises limping along from the day I was born until today, until this moment, all of it parked outside, still following me everywhere, waiting to be told where to go.

Me too, I thought, I'm waiting to be told where to go. Doctor Marlowe wanted to take me to some second chance, some new start full of new hope. She wanted me to believe that the only thing holding me back was myself. She made it sound like I didn't long for a real family and a nice home and nice friends, and I had to be talked into it. Right.

It made me angry just thinking about how she wanted me to blame myself. She expected me to

14

discover what was wrong with me and fix it rather than point to a drunken mother and a deserter and deadbeat for a father. I wasn't ready to excuse them or forget them and it would be a cold day in hell before I would ever forgive them. Granny was right about the hatred gnawing away at my heart, but for now, I didn't see anyplace else for it to be.

Doctor Marlowe's maid Sophie opened the door for me and stepped back quickly as soon as she set her eyes on me. Maybe she thought I had something contagious. The doctor's sister Emma was nowhere in sight, which was fine with me. She was a big, heavy older woman who always looked at me as if she thought I might steal something from the house. I know I made her so nervous she couldn't wait to get out of my sight. I didn't want her there, anyway.

As it turned out, I was the last to arrive. They were all sitting where they had sat yesterday with Doctor Marlowe in her chair. She wore a navy blue dress and had her hair brushed down. I thought it made her look older. Maybe she thought she had to look that way with us. She was tall and lean with long arms and legs. Yesterday, we asked her why she wasn't married, but she wouldn't tell us. She claimed she was the doctor here. She'd do all the asking. It was on the tip of my tongue to say, "You're just hiding behind that like you say we hide behind stuff, too," but I promised Granny I would try not to let my mouth and tongue have a mind of their own.

Jade and Misty glanced at Cat and then at me with self-satisfied smiles on their faces because I had been wrong about her not showing up. After Misty had told her story, I predicted Cat would quit group therapy, but if anything, she looked a little better than she had yesterday. Her hair was neatly brushed. She wore some lipstick and she wore a light-blue cotton dress with loafers. Doctor Marlowe looked pleased about it too. Maybe we were all a good influence on Cat, I thought. At least someone might get something valuable out of this. It was just that I would have guessed Cathy would be the one least likely.

"Good morning, Star," Doctor Marlowe said with a warm smile on her face. Whether she meant it or not, she did make me feel like she was happy to see me.

"Morning."

I took my seat and looked at Misty, who seemed the most anxious of all for me to get started. What did she think I was going to do, I wondered, entertain her?

"It's getting so dark outside," Doctor Marlowe said and turned on another lamp. "We're in for a storm. So? How are you all today?" she asked.

Jade was the only one who really responded.

"Tired," she said with great effort. She was dressed as stylishly as she had been the day before. Today she wore dark blue silk pants with a sash, a ribbed cotton bodysuit and a cardigan sweater tied over her shoulders like some fancy college girl. It all made my red and white dress and scuffed loafers look like some hand-me-downs Granny had found at a thrift shop.

Misty was in jeans and sneakers and wore a T-shirt that said *Mommy went to Paris and all I got was this stupid T-shirt.*

"Still not sleeping well?" Doctor Marlowe asked Jade.

Jade had a way of turning her head so her chin always stayed high. I hated admitting she was pretty, but she was. Those green eyes made her special.

"Nothing's changed," she replied. "Why should I sleep any better?"

Doctor Marlowe nodded. Misty tucked the corner of her mouth into her cheek and Cat stared with admiration at Jade as if she had said the most important thing and was more important than Doctor Marlowe was.

"Anyone want anything before we start?" Doctor Marlowe asked.

"Got milk?" Misty asked with a silly grin. Jade laughed and Cathy the cat smiled. Misty was making fun of the television commercial of course. I couldn't help but snicker myself. At least Misty had some smiles and giggles to carry around as well as the tears and rage. I secretly hoped she had enough for all of us.

"Well, when we take a break, we'll have something," Doctor Marlowe said. She looked at me. "So, today is your day, Star," she said.

"I don't know how to begin," I said, folding my

17

arms under my breasts the way Granny always did when she was setting to hunker down behind an attitude or thought.

"Begin any place you want," Doctor Marlowe said.

"Noplace comes to mind," I said sullenly.

"Do you remember the first time your mother and your father had a bad argument?" Misty asked. "I mean a really bad, all-out argument."

"Maybe she didn't have a father right from the beginning," Jade said in her most arrogant, haughty voice.

I spun on her.

"I had a father," I snapped. "My momma and daddy had a proper wedding and all, too. In a church!"

She shrugged.

"Mine too," she said. "You see all the good that's done me. Now look where I am."

I stared at her for a moment and then gazed at the other two. Each girl seemed to have the same desperate and lost look in her eyes.

It occurred to me that despite our differences, we all had a similar way to say, "Once upon a time."

I guess I could find mine, I thought.

1

"There's no beginning. I don't know as there was ever a time in my house when there wasn't trouble between my momma and daddy," I started. "I saw them be sweet to each other sometimes, but as my granny says, it was like waiting on rainbows after storms. Sometimes the rainbows came, but most of the time not. I think I got so I was surprised to hear them talk to each other without one or the other shouting before they were finished.

"I heard Misty say yesterday that sometimes people get divorced because of money problems. Well, that wasn't the only reason my parents broke up, but it sure didn't help any that my daddy didn't make good money and was out of work often. He was a painter and a carpenter mostly but did other types of work. He could be handy everywhere except around his own house. When he did work, he worked hard, long hours. I think he had a good reputation as far as that goes, but he didn't belong to any unions and he wasn't part of any company that guaranteed him regular work. So there were long periods when times were hard for us and my momma wasn't what you'd call an efficient housewife. I don't know if Daddy would even call her a housewife. He had other names for her and none of them were nice.

"My daddy's a good-looking man, a strapping six-feet four. Anyone would take one look at him and think he must have been a ballplayer in high school, but he always told me he was just too slow to be a good athlete. He said his problem was he thinks too long before he does something. He says he likes being precise and that helps him in all the work he's done as a painter and a carpenter.

"Momma's completely different. She doesn't think so much before she decides to do something. Most of the time, I don't believe she thinks at all. She just does what she wants when she wants. They got into lots of arguments because of that. Daddy said she had a brain that was like a house without any doors. Stuff just went in and out. She'd say she was bound to be on old age Social Security before he did anything worthwhile. Granny used to call them Oil and Water.

"They probably shouldn't have gotten married in the first place, but my momma was pregnant with me before they got married and the way Daddy talked sometimes, I thought he blamed her for all their hard times because of it.

20

If she complained about anything, he would sure always be reminding her that she was the one who had gotten pregnant, as if men could also get pregnant, but had the good sense not to."

Misty laughed and Jade smiled. Cathy smiled too.

"That would be good. That would be fair," Misty said. "At least they would know what it's really like. I know my mother would like that. She'd love to see my father have morning sickness and labor pains."

"Men are babies," Jade declared as if she was standing on the top of some mountain. "If they were the ones who had to get pregnant, the human race would be listed as an endangered species."

We all laughed, including Doctor Marlowe. It made me feel easier about talking, but I still hesitated and looked at Doctor Marlowe for encouragement before I started to talk in great detail about Momma.

It wasn't just because I was ashamed of her, which I had every right to be. Momma had done so many things to make me want to stick my head in the sand. I used to hate to meet up with any friends of mine from school whenever I was with Momma. Not only was there no telling what she would say or do, she usually had bloodshot eyes and smelled like One-Eyed Bill's Bar and Grill down on the southeast corner from our apartment in West Los Angeles. There was a barstool in the place that practically had Momma's name on it. I heard that if she came in and there was someone sitting on it, he or she would just move off and look for another stool — or stand.

When I was just seven, Daddy used to send me to fetch her when he had come home and found she wasn't there making dinner for us. I hated going there, but even then I knew Daddy was sending me because if he had gone instead, they would have had an all-out fight that would turn physical. Daddy would even get into a fight with some other bar customer who felt he had to protect Momma or might even have been flirting with her and wanted to show off.

Sometimes it took so long for me to get her to leave and go home with me, I would start to cry. That usually made her mad because all the other barflies would make fun of her and tell her to go. There was nothing Momma hated more when she drank than anyone telling her what to do. It was like lighting a wick on a dynamite stick. She'd fume and fume and she'd get real nasty and explode into curses and maybe even throw something or swing at someone, especially Daddy, or me for that matter. When Rodney was a baby, I'd have to worry about him crawling around on the kitchen floor because there still might be pieces of plates she had smashed against the wall.

But my hestitation over telling things about her came from another place inside me. Despite what I always told Granny, I hated hating Momma. Mixed with all the bad memories were lots of good ones. There were many times when she had held me and had sung to me and had fixed my hair and kissed me. She used to call me her Precious and she used to dream big dreams for me. All those memories were planted in someplace special in my heart too, and I couldn't help feeling like I was betraying them when I told about all the bad things.

For now, though, that seemed to be what Doctor Marlowe wanted me to do. From the way she talked about it, holding the bad down was like trying to keep poison in your body.

"I can't remember exactly when my momma started drinking," I began, "but it was always a lot and it was always bad, especially for me and my brother Rodney."

They all lost their smiles and their eyes became hard and cold like the eyes of those who had seen terrible things happen and knew what I was going through in just talking about it, for there was no way to talk about it without reliving it. Remembering made me a five-year-old girl again, brought back all the demons, all the dark shadows that haunted my bedroom after something awful had happened between Momma and Daddy.

The monsters were a part of me now, dormant, lying around and waiting to be nudged by the sound of someone shouting, by the sight of some poor child playing in the gutter because his mother was neglecting him, by the wail of ambulance sirens or police sirens, or merely by the sounds of someone crying in the darkness, someone as alone and afraid as I had been and maybe forever would be.

"When I think back on it now, it seems to me that there was always a lot of drinking going on. Momma smelled from it so much, I used to think it was a kind of perfume she wore," I said.

Misty laughed.

"Of course, I wasn't very old when I thought that.

"Sometimes, she would just let me stand there by the door and pretend she didn't know who I was. I was afraid to call to her. I knew how mad that made her. Finally, she would look at Bill and say, 'My ball and chain is home from work,' and they would all cackle and tease her, and she would blame me.

" 'Why did he have to send you here?' she would snap at me.

" 'He wants you to come home and make us supper, Momma,' I would tell her and she would shake her head and mimic me.

"She'd stare at herself in the mirror behind the bar for a few moments and then finish her beer in a gulp and get up a little wobbly.

" 'What's for dinner, Aretha?' someone would shout.

" 'My heart,' she'd scream back and whoever was there would laugh and laugh. 'Go on,' Momma would tell me. 'Get outta here. You made enough trouble for me.'

"I'd wait for her on the sidewalk. Sometimes

she'd come right out and sometimes, she'd start up again and I'd have to go back inside and then she'd come.

"Usually she wouldn't say much as we walked home, but when she did it was almost always about what a big mistake her whole life was.

" 'That man who calls himself your father promised me Easy Street,' she'd claim. 'He said we'd live in a nice house in a nice neighborhood and I'd have a yard for a garden like my momma has. Not some rat hole four-room dump that it doesn't even pay to clean. You wipe the dust off the table and it just floats back a few minutes later. I told him why bother with it when he complained about my housekeeping.'

"She'd stop and look at herself in a store window and maybe make a small effort to fix her hair and straighten her dress. It was funny how no matter what happened between her and Daddy, Momma always wanted to be pretty for him.

"Momma's about five feet six. No matter how much she drank, she didn't seem to lose her figure. She never grew those big hips many women her age got from eating and drinking the worst stuff. Daddy would say all the booze went to her head and soaked her brain instead. I always thought she was pretty and only looked ugly when she got real drunk. Her lower lip sags and her eyes droop. Daddy told her he couldn't stand looking at her when she was like that, and one time, when they had an all-out slam-bam, he put a pillowcase over her head and tied it at her neck so that she spun about and whipped her arms wildly, knocking things over, falling over a chair, and kicking like some wild animal."

Cat's mouth was wide open. Jade looked like she might throw up and Misty bit down on her lower lip and looked at Doctor Marlowe. It occurred to me that their parents probably only threw nasty words and threats at each other and probably mostly through their expensive attorneys. Most likely, they couldn't even imagine their mothers and fathers trying to do physical harm to each other. The stuff I was telling them and was about to tell them, they saw only in the movies or on television.

"That wasn't the worst thing," I said, "but my daddy was generally an easy-going man."

"Easy-going?" Jade asked snidely.

"I can't recall him ever lifting his hand to threaten me or my brother Rodney, but when my momma got real drunk so that she slobbered and cursed and called him all kinds of dirty names, he lost control of himself, that's all.

"Once, when I was still only about five, I remember him trying to scare her by smashing a plate on the floor. She went even wilder on him, however, and scooped out cups and saucers, glasses and bowls from the cabinet, sending them flying every which way and screaming 'You want to see something break, Kenny Fisher? I'll show you something break.'

"The only way he could stop her was to wrap

his arms around her and hold her down. She tried kicking at him and even tried to get her head down low enough to bite his arm. She'd bitten him plenty of times before, but he's a strong man and he lifted her and carried her to their bedroom where he threw her on the bed and practically sat on her while she flared about, slapping at him, until she grew exhausted and passed out.

"When he came out of the bedroom, he had scratches on his neck and his arms that were still bleeding. I was too scared to move. In fact," I said glancing at Doctor Marlowe, "I think I peed in my pants."

The others were gaping at me as if I was something from out of space. You all asked for it, I thought, well, I'll give it to you.

"I had that problem for a long time after I was supposed to. Momma even took me to the doctor once and he told her it was all in my head. She got mad at him and called him stupid because it was all in my panties not in my head. He wanted me to go see a psychiatrist back then and Momma called him nuts and dragged me out of the office, screaming she wasn't going to pay no quack a penny. She vowed she'd cure me and her way was to force me to wear wet panties, even when Daddy complained about the stink."

"Ugh," Jade moaned. "That's disgusting. Can I get a glass of water or something, Doctor Marlowe?"

"Sure. How about the rest of you?" She smiled

at Misty. "Want milk?"

"No thanks," she said quickly, looking like she was holding breakfast down. "I'll just have water, too."

"All right. Let me get a pitcher of ice water for now. It's so humid, isn't it?" Doctor Marlowe looked at me and I thought she looked pleased. I guess she wanted me to shake up our little group after all.

She rose. Cathy said she had to go to the bathroom and left with her. Jade and Misty turned to me.

"Do you see your mother much anymore?" Misty asked.

"No. I'll talk about all that when they return," I said. "Otherwise I'll just be repeating myself and these things aren't things I like to talk about, much less repeat."

She nodded. They were both quiet for a moment, but I could see Jade's mind working.

"It's not really my business," she said softly, "but under the circumstances, how can your grandmother afford Doctor Marlowe? I mean, I know what it's costing my parents," she added, looking to Misty, who nodded.

"The court told some agency to pay for it. I don't know all the details, but no one asks me or my granny for any money. If they did, I wouldn't come back. That's for sure. We got better places for Granny's money."

They both looked sorry for me.

"Don't worry about me," I told them sharply.

"I'm not looking for anyone's pity or charity and I'd really rather not come here, but I got to."

They both nodded, trying not to look too sympathetic so I wouldn't get mad at them.

Cat returned first and avoided my eyes.

"You look nice today," Misty told her. "You oughta cut your bangs, though."

"You have split ends, too," Jade told her. "Where do you go to get your hair done?"

"My mother does my hair," Cat said.

"So, just tell her to trim it more," Misty said with a shrug.

She ain't so bad, I thought. At least she don't seem as stuck up.

Doctor Marlowe set the tray with a jug of ice water and glasses on the table.

"I've got a surprise for you all today," she said. "Since we started a little later this morning, I decided it would be nice if we had a real lunch break, so I'm having some pizzas brought in."

"Maybe I won't take that long," I suggested.

"Then Jade will get started," Doctor Marlowe quickly replied. Cat looked relieved knowing she didn't have to be next. When her turn came, she would definitely fail to show up, I thought.

Doctor Marlowe poured everyone a glass of water. Then she nodded at me to continue.

"When I was nearly nine years old, Momma got pregnant again," I said. "I thought she was never going to have another baby. She had kept from getting pregnant for a long time. I didn't know it until much later, but Momma had been pregnant before. She had lost a baby when I was only two, lost it in our bathtub."

The three of them froze in anticipation of me describing how. I thought about it for a few moments and decided not to. When I talked about the next pregnancy instead, they looked very relieved. It almost made me laugh out loud. I was beginning to enjoy the grimaces, looks of shock and disgust on their faces.

Doctor Marlowe could see that in my face, too. She gave me a look that told me so and I wiped the smug smile off my face quickly.

"For a little while after my momma became pregnant, things settled down in our house. Momma actually cut back on her drinking because the doctor told her she could hurt the baby. She did a better job of cleaning our house. She cooked again and Daddy got more work. We had a little money and did some nice things together, like taking trips to Magic Mountain and once to Knott's Berry Farm. We went to visit Daddy's cousin Leonard in San Diego, too, and went to the zoo.

"Momma was pretty big by this time. Sometimes, Rodney would kick in her stomach and she'd call me to put my hand on it and feel him. We didn't know it was a boy yet, but I got so I was excited someone was coming. I thought it would be fun to have a little baby in the house and to help look after him or her. Little did I know just how much looking after I would eventually have to do."

"A lot?" Misty asked.

I stared at her for a moment.

"Sometimes, I thought he thought I was his mother instead of his sister."

"Terrible," Jade said. "Putting that sort of responsibility on you when you were so young."

"Yeah, well, what you have to do, you do unless you got all kinds of servants to do it for you," I told her.

She looked away.

"When Momma was about in her seventh month, Daddy got laid off again and we had to watch every penny. Momma just hated that. It made her more wasteful just for spite. I guess it was her way of telling Daddy he'd better find new work soon. She wasn't going to deny herself anything, especially her cigarettes or occasional beer.

"One night soon after, while Daddy was trying to find some work, she went to One-Eyed Bill's. When he came home and found she was gone, he went into a rage and this time he didn't send me to go fetch her. After all, she was pregnant and she wasn't supposed to be drinking, so he went himself, nearly ripping the door off its hinges when he charged out of our apartment.

"At One-Eyed Bill's he hit a man who came between him and Momma and the police had to come. I'll never forget that," I said and looked down at the floor. The memory put ice around my heart for a moment.

"I was just sitting in the living room watching

31

television and looking at the door every once in a while, terrified of what Momma was going to be like coming through it when I heard a knock and then saw a policewoman and a policeman. The policewoman was black.

"She knew my name and all and told me she had come to be sure I was all right. Daddy had told her I was here. She said I'd have to go with them for a while and I shook my head and started to cry. I even tried to run away from them, but they caught me and made me go with them to the police station. I remember thinking I'm being arrested for being Momma's daughter because she was so bad."

I looked up. The three girls were staring at me, none of them taking a breath.

"They kept me in a room and gave me hot chocolate and cookies while they waited to see what was going to happen to Daddy and Momma. She had torn up some of the bar, too, but One-Eyed Bill didn't press any charges and Daddy was released pending a court appearance. The other man didn't show up and they dropped all the charges against Daddy, but it was enough to put a little scare into Momma.

"She behaved herself for quite a while afterward and then Rodney was born in the bathroom."

"What did you say?" Jade immediately asked. Her head spun around at me so fast, I thought it might keep going around and around on her neck.

"Daddy wasn't home," I continued, ignoring her. "It was the middle of the afternoon. I had just come back from school. I was in the fifth grade by then. I came into the apartment and called for Momma like always, only she didn't call back. I looked for her in her bedroom and I saw she wasn't there. Then I heard her scream and I ran to the bathroom.

"She was on the floor and I could see the baby coming. The sight nailed my feet to the floor. She was yelling for me to go get help, to call nine-one-one. I started crying. I couldn't help it and she kept screaming and yelling at me. Finally, I went to the phone and called and told the operator my momma was having a baby on the bathroom floor. I gave her our address and hung up. Then I heard Rodney cry and when I looked back in the bathroom, Momma had him on her stomach, but there was blood and the afterbirth and . . ."

"Oh, my God, do we have to listen to this?" Jade cried with her mouth twisting into a grimace of disgust.

Cathy looked a shade whiter than milk. Misty sat with her eyes wide, her mouth dropped so that I could practically see what she had for breakfast.

"I don't want you to be upset, Jade, but you should know what Star's life is really like and when your turn comes, you shouldn't hold anything back for fear of upsetting the others either."

"Like I have something that gross to tell," Jade replied, swinging those green eyes toward the ceiling.

"What might not be as disagreeable to you, could be to Star."

"Oh please."

"Why don't you put your fingers in your ears?" I told her.

She looked like she was going to say something back, but held off.

"Just finish describing what happened, Star," Doctor Marlowe commanded.

"She asked me to fetch her a towel and I did and then I got some hot water for her and we waited. The paramedics came and finished off Rodney's birth, but they took them both to the hospital just the same. Granny came to be with me and finally Daddy showed up and saw Rodney and Momma. She was all right, but mad as hell at him for not being there. They had another argument in the hospital, Daddy defending himself for being out looking for a job and Momma screaming about how she almost died giving birth to his son.

"Right from the start, she made it sound like Rodney was only his and she was just delivering him. That way she blamed Daddy for all the work and all the problems, starting right then and there. The nurse had to ask them to stop yelling.

"Momma and Rodney stayed only that night. I went home with Granny and she brought me

34

back the next day. It was one thing to see Rodney behind that window in the hospital, but quite another to see him in his little crib beside Momma and Daddy's bed. I thought the sight of him was a wonder. His head didn't look much bigger than one of my rubber balls and when he cried, he lifted his small, puffy arms and waved his tiny fists in the air like he was looking for someone or something to punch. I stood there for long periods of time watching him breathe and then wake up and scream, taking a breath and then throwing out this shrill little cry.

"The only thing that seemed to quiet him was Momma putting his mouth on her nipple."

"Oh, my God," Jade muttered, but both Cathy and Misty looked fascinated. "Are you going to describe breast-feeding in great detail?"

"Scare you?" I fired back at her.

"It doesn't scare me, but I'm not going to do it."

"My mother didn't do it," Misty said. "She had read where it could scar her breast and she could lose shape. What about your mother?" she asked Cathy.

Cat shook her head vigorously.

"I don't know," she said in a voice just above a whisper.

"You never asked?" Misty pursued.

"No," she said. She looked like she would get up and run out of the room if Misty didn't stop.

"It's a natural thing to be curious about,"

Misty muttered, not wanting to look bad for asking.

"It's not necessary to know," Jade insisted. "It's like hearing about someone's bowel movements."

"It is not!"

"I hope that's not next," Jade muttered without looking at me.

"I guess we know where her hang-ups are," Misty said.

"You don't know anything about me!" Jade cried. "What right do you have to judge me?"

"Girls," Doctor Marlowe said calmly, "this is not going to be productive if you don't show each other at least a minimum of respect. No one here has had it easy, but if you don't give each other a chance to be as open as possible, you won't help each other."

Jade didn't look convinced, but she relaxed in her seat and Misty looked sorry.

"From the way my granny talked about a new baby, I always thought we would become a happy family when Rodney was born, but Momma only complained about our lives more and more. Daddy got new work, but now he was never making enough money for us. When they argued and shouted at each other, I heard her blame him for Rodney all the time, claiming he was the one who wanted a son. She talked like she didn't want him and when I looked at my little brother, I couldn't imagine anyone, least of all his own momma, not wanting him.

"He was a colicky baby. Nothing seemed to help. He did cry a lot and Momma would rage about the apartment, complaining that the doctor didn't know nothing and she would go mad. She made Daddy get up with Rodney every night, no matter how early in the morning he had to go to work. When she saw I could help, really help, could hold Rodney safely, get him to drink his bottle and rock him to sleep, even if it was only for a little while, she started to keep me home from school more often. She did it so much, the school truant officer came by and when he saw I wasn't really sick, he threatened the school would take Momma to court and maybe take me away from her.

"I heard her mumble, 'Take them both.'

"Maybe she said it because she was frustrated and tired, but it hurt to hear it. It felt like it burned into my brain. I thought it might really happen, too. I had trouble sleeping and every time someone came to our door, my heart would race for fear it was someone to come take both Rodney and me away and put us in some institution.

"Granny came by often as she could, but she and Momma got into arguments about the way Momma kept the house and how she took care of Rodney. She knew Momma was starting to drink again, too.

"By this time, Momma was hiding booze all over the house. She was drinking vodka because it didn't smell as bad and she had it in shampoo bottles and even in a hot water bag she kept in the closet. For months and months, Daddy didn't discover it, but soon she became sloppy about hiding it and he would find a glass of orange juice or cranberry juice and taste it and know she had vodka in it.

"When he complained, she screamed about how hard her life was with two children to look after, one being a twenty-four-hour responsibility. Of course, she brought up money problems continually, and then he would accuse her of wasting what little we had on her booze habit. She claimed it was the only thing keeping her sane and he said if she was sane, then he didn't know what crazy meant anymore.

"I'd come home from school and find Rodney lying there in unchanged diapers. From the rashes and irritation on his legs and little behind, I knew he had been like that almost all day. Of course, that made him scream and cry more which sent Momma to the bottle more. She got so she could sleep right through him wailing away. I guess she was really more passed out than sleeping. I'd find her everywhere like that, even on the floor in her bedroom sometimes."

"She should have been locked up," Jade said.

I stared at her for a long moment and then I looked out the window at the drizzle that had begun. Maybe Jade was right, but it hurt to have someone else say it.

There were lots of worse things in life that could and maybe would happen to us, but hating your own mother had to be at the top of the list.

"She's right," I told Doctor Marlowe, "but I don't want her to be."

"I know," she said softly. "That's why you're all here: to find an alternative to hate."

"Why do we need to?" Misty asked with that little sarcastic turn in her lips.

"Because I think you all know by now, that you can't hate your parents without hating your-selves."

No one had to agree out loud. We could just look into each other's eyes and see that Doctor Marlowe was right.

2

"When Rodney began to crawl and then stand, things got worse because he was a curious baby from the start and he would get into places and things in a flash. One afternoon, I came home and found Momma had left him alone while she went out to get herself a couple of six-packs of beer. I guess he was asleep when she had left and she thought he'd be all right. I didn't know it, but she had left him alone many times before and once when she was with a girlfriend, Maggie Custer, they had left him in Maggie's car and a policeman had seen it and nearly arrested her.

"Anyway, this time Rodney woke up, crawled out of the cot-bed we now had for him and went looking for her. He wandered into the bathroom where Momma had left some of his rubber toys in the tub. There wasn't any water in the tub or he'd'a drowned for sure because he managed to fall into it when he tried to get to his toys. He hit his head on the faucet, I suppose. At first I thought Momma had taken him out with her because it was so quiet, but when I walked into the bathroom, I nearly jumped out of my skin. There he was lying on his back very still, his eyes wild and full of terror. I found out later that a head wound usually bleeds a lot, but at the time it turned my heart to stone. I saw all the blood around his head and I started screaming. I was familiar with calling nine-one-one by now. I told the operator my little brother had fallen and put a hole in his head. It didn't turn out to be that bad, but he did need ten stitches.

"The paramedics were there before Momma returned. She met one of her barfly friends who had talked her into just one drink at One-Eyed Bill's and she just forgot how much time went by, I imagine.

"The paramedics took him to the hospital emergency room where the doctor sewed up Rodney's wound. The paramedics wanted to know everything while a policeman went to fetch Momma. I had to tell them what had happened and they looked at each other angrily. When Momma arrived, she was fit to be tied that I had called them because they pulled her aside and gave her a what-for that spun her eyes. They threatened to tell the police and have someone from the Child Protection Service on her back if she let something like this happen again. They even told her she could go to jail for endangering the life of an infant.

"After we all got brought home, Momma started on me. Daddy came home right in the middle of it, saw Rodney and heard enough bits and pieces to realize what had occurred. I guess he knew about some of the other times, but he didn't get as wildly angry as I had expected he would.

"Instead, he got all quiet, this strange mood coming over him as if he was a clam or something and just closed up his shell. He looked at me and at Rodney and just sat with his eyes glazed while Momma went on and on like a worn CD, repeating her same complaints and trying to excuse herself.

" 'Who do they think they are telling me I'm not a good mother just because I stepped out for a moment? Huh? Who knew he'd get up and walk himself into the bathroom and fall into the tub, huh? I'm no fortune teller. I was coming right back. He was asleep. Who do they think they are reading me the riot act, huh?

" 'Why are you just sitting there staring into space like that, Kenny? What's this act supposed to be. You trying to make me feel bad? You know what it's like being stuck here with an infant all day? I'm talking to you. I'm looking at you and I'm talking to you.'

"Daddy said nothing. Still looking dazed, he just got up suddenly and walked out of the apartment. Momma stood there with her hands on her hips, her mouth wide and her eyes blazing. He closed the door softly behind him.

"She turned to me and said, 'Did you see that? Did you?'

"My heart was thumping like a parade drum. I couldn't speak or swallow.

" 'Of all the raw nerve . . . Well, good riddance to you too!' she screamed at the door. Then she opened it, stuck her head out in the hallway and screamed it again, but he was already out of the building.

"I saw my daddy only once after that."

"Saw him only once? What do you mean? Your father just left you and Rodney for good?" Jade asked, practically jumping out of her seat.

It was funny, but while I was telling them about it all, I really did forget they were there. Something like this had happened before, of course, but usually only with Doctor Marlowe. My memories would get so thick, they'd block out the present, where I was and what I was doing. I felt like I had fallen back and I was really there again. Momma's angry face was so vivid in my mind, those eyes bloodshot, her mouth twisted and her shoulders hoisted making her look like some kind of wild bird about to pounce.

Whenever she went into her ranting, my stomach would close like a fist and my breath would catch in my throat, making me feel as though I could choke on air. Retelling these bad times put me back into that state of mind and I wouldn't snap out of it until my lungs screamed. I'd blink a lot and realize where I was and I'd be grateful I wasn't back then.

That's how I felt now when Jade blurted her question at me. I looked at her for a few moments without realizing who she was and where I was. Her face got all twisted with confusion.

"Why doesn't she answer me, Doctor Marlowe? Why is she just staring at me like that?" I heard her ask.

"Star?" Doctor Marlowe said. "Star?"

That was my name, I thought. I heard her, but she sounded like she was at the other end of a long tunnel.

"Doctor Marlowe?" Misty said. "She looks spaced."

"She'll be all right, girls. Relax. Don't let her feel your panic. Star, honey?"

"Star, honey," Granny was calling. "You got to go to school, child, or they won't let you stay here with me. You know what that judge told us. Get up now, honey. C'mon, child. Wake up. Your eyes are open, Star. Wake up!"

I felt my body shake.

"Star, come on. You're not there; you're here," Doctor Marlowe said.

My face felt cool. She was dabbing me with a wet napkin.

"That's it. You'll be fine, Star. Come on. Stay with us."

She took my hand and squeezed it gently. My eyelids were fluttering like butterflies in a panic and then they slowed and I looked into Doctor Marlowe's eyes. They were moving over my face like two tiny searchlights. She smiled.

"There you are. You're fine," she said.

I looked at the others. They were all staring at me, each of them looking more shocked and afraid than the other.

"What is it?" I asked.

"Nothing. You drifted off a bit," Doctor Marlowe said. "It's no big deal. No problem. You're fine. Here, take some water," she said offering me my glass. I sipped some and took a deep breath.

"I forgot what I was saying," I said. My memories were jumbled like a can of alphabet soup.

Doctor Marlowe smiled and sat back.

"Well, you were telling us about the time your father got up and walked out of the house," she said. She made it sound as if it was just another part of the story, nothing terribly serious. Her voice had a calming effect.

I nodded.

"He didn't say good-bye to me or nothing," I muttered.

"That's right," Doctor Marlowe said as if she had been there with me.

I looked at her and realized in a way she had because I had told her about this before, many times before, and I always had trouble going on after that.

The others were still staring at me, their eyes so unmoving they could have been glass.

"Why're you all looking at me like that?" I snapped.

Jade smirked.

"She's fine," she said and sat back. "She can go on and on," she added.

"It's not that easy," Misty said. "Just because I did it yesterday, doesn't mean it was simple and it will be simple for you or for her or for Cat."

"Don't tell me how it's going to be for me," Jade fired back at her.

"I'm just trying to be . . ."

"What? Another Doctor Marlowe? One's enough," Jade quipped and turned away.

"Well. At least we're not boring each other," Doctor Marlowe said. Jade made some sound under her breath. Cat looked from one of us to the other, her eyes still full of terror.

"Try to go on, Star," Doctor Marlowe urged. "Tell them the rest of it," she urged as if it was more important for them to hear it than for me to get it out.

Jade turned her head slowly toward me to see what I was going to do. Almost for spite, I continued.

"I just saw him once after that time. I didn't speak to him. I was on my way home from school. It was just starting to rain and I saw him come out of our apartment building carrying some of his things and walking quickly toward his truck. I sped up and called to him. I know he heard me because I saw him slow down even though he didn't turn his head. He looked down at the sidewalk and then sped up again until he reached his truck.

"I was running by now, thinking maybe he

didn't realize it was me calling to him, but I couldn't get to him before he started the truck and pulled away from the curb. With all my might, I shouted.

" 'Daddy! Daddy!' I stopped when my lungs were ready to burst, my ribs aching, and I watched the truck go down to the next corner, turn and disappear. The rain came down harder and harder so I had to go inside. You couldn't tell the difference between my tears and the raindrops streaking down my face."

"What happened to him? Where did he go?" Misty asked, her eyebrows knitted with concern.

"Momma heard stories that he was with another woman and he went north to San Francisco, but I never knew if the stories were just some gossip or what."

"Your father just picked up and deserted you and your brother? That's what you're telling us?" Jade asked, still sounding skeptical.

"He wasn't the first husband and Daddy to do that," I told her. I looked at them. "Your parents deserted you, too. They just did it more respectfully or, what word did you use yesterday, Misty, civilly? Something like that anyway," I said.

"Isn't that against the law?" Jade asked Doctor Marlowe. "What her father did?"

"Well, Star's father would be what we call a deadbeat dad and yes, what he's done is against the law," she replied. "There's even a federal law against that now."

"Did your mother have him arrested?" Jade followed.

"She went down to welfare and reported her situation so she could get some money, but it didn't get put at the top of anyone's list. It wasn't exactly what you would call a high priority," I said.

"Men are creeps," Jade muttered.

"My momma ain't exactly an angel," I told her. Her eyebrows lifted.

"What happened to her?"

"Why don't you give her a chance to tell it her own way?" Misty asked Jade.

"I'm sorry," she said. "It just makes me . . . mad."

I widened my eyes.

"It doesn't exactly put joy in my heart either," I said.

Jade's lips stretched into a tight smile. Damned if I didn't know whether I should hate her or like her.

"Momma didn't realize Daddy was gone for good that first night he walked out on us, of course. She made us some supper and sat drinking her beer all night and watching television. I put Rodney to bed. He was groggy and tired from his ordeal, but he was still in some pain. The paramedics had instructed us to give him some Tylenol, which I did. I sang a little to him and his eyes slowly closed.

"After he had fallen asleep, I went out and sat with Momma and watched television awhile, hoping Daddy would come home while I was still up, but he didn't. Finally, exhausted myself, I went to sleep.

"As soon as my eyes snapped open the next morning, I hopped out of bed and looked in on Momma and Daddy's bedroom, expecting to see his long, lanky body stretched over the comforter, his arm dangling over the side as usual. He usually ended up on the cover instead of under it.

"Momma had fallen asleep with her clothes still on and was spread-eagle, alone, breathing through her mouth and looking like she had been put into a trance. Rodney, who still slept next to them on his cot-bed, was sitting up, playing quietly with one of his toys. He looked happy when he saw me looking in on him.

"My heart felt like a Yo-Yo whose string had broken. All night it had gone up and down with every sound in the building that suggested Daddy's return. Now, it was clear he hadn't come back and I was sick with fear.

"I took Rodney into the living room and fixed him some breakfast. Momma woke up looking dazed and confused as usual after a night of drinking. She was surprised to see Daddy hadn't returned, too.

" 'Where'd Daddy go?' I asked her.

" 'How would I know? Who cares?' she said, but it bothered her when he didn't return the next day. She got on the phone and complained to Granny and then two days after that, she

49

started to call some of Daddy's friends and I guess she found out he had left Los Angeles. That was when she went to welfare and cried about our situation.

"For a long time, I expected Daddy would come back, even after I saw him that last time and he hurried away from me. I never told Momma I had seen him. I knew it would just make her wild and angry and after a while, I began to wonder if I had really seen him or just imagined it out of hope. Whenever the phone rang, I hoped it was him calling, but it never was. Momma was so furious she would swear she wasn't going to take him back if he did show up, but I knew in my heart she would.

"Granny started to spend more time with us soon after all that. She lives in Venice Beach so it was a trip for her. When I would go to see her, I'd have to ride the Big Blue Bus for nearly two hours to make the right connections and you know the buses don't run that often."

I glanced at them.

"Well, you girls probably don't know 'cause you probably never been on a Big Blue Bus in Los Angeles, have you?"

"I have," Cat blurted. She looked like she had confessed to a crime or something. "My mother didn't know I did, but I did," she added.

"How'd you like it?" I asked her.

"It was all right," she said. "Nobody bothered me."

"Why should they? Just because someone

don't have enough money to have his or her own car don't mean they're rapists and serial killers, you know."

"I was just scared," she said. She said it with such honesty, I couldn't harden my heart against her for it.

"Yeah, well, I've been scared on the bus too," I admitted, "especially at night.

"But I often had to ride it then because I would have stayed at Granny's too long and I didn't want her to have to drive me home in the dark. Her eyes weren't so good back then and they are even worse now.

"I got so I ran to Granny every so often because I couldn't stand coming home from school and finding Momma drinking, Rodney still in his pajamas, and the house looking like ten slobs lived in it. Granny knew why I showed up at her house in the afternoon from time to time, but she didn't harp on it. She had tried and tried with Momma and finally just threw up her hands and declared, 'My Aretha's just one of those people who have to decide to help themselves because they won't let anyone else do it.

" 'Your momma will wake up facedown in the gutter one day and maybe then she'll decide to do something about herself,' Granny told me.

"She told it to me so often, I began to wish for it, wish I would come home and find Momma outside facedown in the street. I suppose it don't say much for you when all you can hope for is your momma hitting rock bottom sooner than later, but that's how it was and I'm not ashamed of praying for it.

"That's right," I said glaring at them before they could gasp or ask some stupid question, "I did pray for it. I went to sleep asking God to send my momma close to hell as soon as He had the opportunity.

"So yes, I did get so I hated her. At times it was like a rat of hatred was gnawing at my heart. I probably will always hate her," I declared firmly.

No one said a word. It was as if we were all in freeze-frame, not a movement, not even the sound of anyone breathing.

"Not having Daddy home even once in a while was like taking a leash off a dog as far as Momma was concerned. She didn't have to worry about him coming back from work and not finding her in the house. She didn't care what the house looked like either, since he wasn't there to criticize and complain. At first, it was like her way of getting even with him for leaving her. I could almost hear her say, 'He thought I was a no-good drunk slob before? Well, he should see me now.'

"I stayed home from school even more because after I saw to Rodney, it was often very late in the morning and I'd have missed the first two classes by the time I got there.

"Then Momma went and did the worst thing of all: she got herself a night job at One-Eyed Bill's waitressing and helping out in the kitchen.

"By then I was able to make dinner for Rodney and me, and I cleaned the house and did most all the chores. That's why I told you earlier that it got so my little brother didn't know who was his mother and who was his sister.

"Momma was supposed to always be home by one o'clock, but there were many nights when I know she didn't come home until three or four. She'd be so dead out of it in the morning, I could drop a frying pan next to her bed and she wouldn't as much as bat an eyelash. Lots of nights she was too drunk or tired to bother getting out of her clothes. She smelled so bad from beer and whiskey, the whole bedroom reeked like a One-Eyed Bill's. The stench would reach through the walls into my room. I'd have to open all the windows in the place."

"Ugh," Misty said holding her stomach. Jade swallowed hard and turned away for a moment, pressing the back of her hand against her mouth. I couldn't blame them.

"You get used to it," I muttered. "You'd never dream you would, but you do. There ain't much else you can do, but turn the other way most of the time."

"I understand," Cat said in a quivering small voice. She was holding her attention on me.

"You do? That's good, because I don't," I said. She just continued to stare, but I felt she was looking at her own memories now, not mine. After a moment she seemed to snap out of it and look down again.

"Granny came by often to help out and occasionally make us a real good dinner," I continued. "She and Momma had some big fights, but Momma would wail and claim she was doing the best she could, deserted by a husband and left with two kids to raise and support.

" 'Why do you think that man left you?' Granny would ask her and that would be the same as lighting that wick again. Momma would go wild, her arms and legs and even her head swinging so hard, I thought they might just fly off her body and bounce against the wall along with her screams.

" 'How can my own mother blame me for that rotten man? Why is it always my fault? He was the one who made all them promises, wasn't he? I did the best I could with the little money he brought us. Lots a times he brought us nothin' because he was out of work so much. It's no loss him bein' gone, no ma'am.'

"On and on she would go and I'd listen and wonder if she really believed the things she said. Maybe her eyes saw differently. Maybe she was just a step or two off-center and her world was running on a different track, you know. She always looked so satisfied with herself after one of those explosions of temper, like she had made important points and shut everyone up. That's when I began to understand what was meant when someone said 'You're only fooling yourself.' Momma really was fooling herself. She truly believed she was the victim and not us, not even me and Rodney. We were . . . just unfortunate enough to be born.

"Like I said, I guess no matter what your life is like, you can get used to it and just accept things as they are. Of course, I knew other girls my age didn't have this kind of life. Oh, they helped out with their little brothers and sisters, but their little brothers and sisters didn't become their children. They still thought about boys and parties and going to the movies and having fun. I couldn't think of anything without thinking about Rodney being a part of it. I didn't have a night off, so to speak," I said. "I was afraid of bringing anyone to my house. I didn't want my friends at school to know just how bad things were for me and for Rodney.

"Then," I said, taking a sip of water and thinking for a moment, "then I got so I could live through their stories. Their lives became my life. It was easier to pretend, to imagine my name was Lily Porter or Charlene Davis and in my mind go home to their houses and live with their families.

"You're all looking at me like I was crazy. Well, maybe I was for a while. Doctor Marlowe says I'm not crazy now."

"No one's crazy here, Star. It's an inappropriate word, a meaningless word," she said.

"Yeah, maybe, but I sure wasn't in my right mind. I did some things," I said. After a moment, I added, "Things I haven't even told you yet, Doctor Marlowe.

"Whenever I met someone who didn't know me, for example, I would give them a phony

55

name, one of the names of the girls I envied and I would talk like I was Lily Porter or Charlene Davis, describing their homes and their families as if they really were mine.

"A couple of times, I went to Charlene Davis's house, walked right up to the door, pretending I was coming home. One time, I nearly got caught doing it. Her sister Lori came up behind me without me knowing and asked me what I was doing.

" 'I was just going to see if your sister was home,' I said. She looked at me sideways because she knew I knew her sister was on the cheerleading team and would be at practice. I made believe I forgot and walked away quickly. When Charlene asked me about it the next day, I said I was just in her neighborhood and had to kill some time. She didn't believe me. They all started looking at me as if I was funny.

"I couldn't help it. I wanted their lives so much I'd follow their mothers around a supermarket, pretending I was with them, buying food.

"You think I was pretty pathetic, don't you?" I asked Jade.

"No," she said. "Really," she added, when I looked skeptical. "I can understand not wanting to be who you are. I've felt like that lots of times."

"Me too," Misty said.

"Yes," Cat said. "Me too." She looked like she meant it more than any of us. How could her story be worse than mine? I wondered.

"There's more," I said, now willing to tell it all.

"One time I hurt my ankle in gym class and the teacher sent me back to the locker room to get dressed. I noticed Charlene's locker was unlocked and I opened it and took her blouse."

"Why?" Jade asked with a grimace.

"To wear it later, when I was alone at home in my room. I pretended I was her and I lived in a nice house with a real mother and a father. Her daddy works for the city. He's some kind of traffic manager, makes good money, and her mother always looks stylish. They come to the basketball games and watch her cheer for the team. She's about my size, too, so the blouse fit real good."

"What happened when she found her blouse was missing?" Misty asked. "Did they accuse you?"

"No. The teacher made everyone open her locker and she looked in all of them."

"How come they didn't find it in yours? Where did you put it?"

"I didn't put it in my locker," I said. "I told you I wanted to take it home with me so I hid it under my skirt and no one dared look there. They just thought someone had come into the locker room and robbed it. Things like that had happened before. Charlene had to wear her gym uniform top for the rest of the day.

"About a month or so afterward, I brought it back and left it on the bench near her locker. Everyone thought it was weird. It was weird," I admitted.

"No it wasn't," Cat piped up. Everyone looked at her. She didn't hide her face this time.

"Why not?"

"I don't just want to be in someone else's clothes; I want to be in their bodies," she confessed.

Everyone was quiet. The air felt so heavy and even with the lights, a thick shadow seemed to hang over the ceiling and walls.

"Well," Doctor Marlowe said. "Why don't I go check on the pizza for us? It's getting close to that time."

She rose and looked at me.

"I guess you'll continue after lunch, right?"

I nodded and she left us. As soon as she had, Jade turned to me.

"I'm sorry I was nasty to you before," she said and then quickly added, "and I'm not trying to show you any pity so don't get mad at me."

"It's all right," I said. "About now, I could use some, I suppose."

"I suppose we all can," Misty said.

"As long as we don't depend on it," I said. "It's a little scarce outside this place. My granny says if you wait too long for pity, you'll miss the train to happiness."

They all smiled, even Cat. Everyone looked a lot more comfortable. It was like we were all trying each other on for size, making adjustments here and there and finding ways to make it work.

"Your granny sounds like a wise old lady," Jade said.

"She is. Well, I guess I am hungry," I said. "Least we'll get something out of this, lunch. I hope I didn't spoil anyone's appetite."

"Not mine!" Misty blurted and put her hand over her mouth.

And then we all laughed.

It felt good, like some of that sunshine after the storm Granny always expected.

3

Doctor Marlowe had a table set up for us in her closed-in back patio. There were large windows facing the pool and yard and a sliding door. It was still raining lightly, the drops zigzagging to outline odd shapes on the glass. Birds flitted from tree to tree, probably excited by the sight of worms that had come out of the dampened earth. The birds were about to enjoy a little feast too, I thought. When I caught sight of my reflection in the glass, I saw I had a smile on my face. It happened so rarely these days, it took me by surprise and I touched my cheek as if to be sure it was me.

I don't often look at birds, I thought. I know they are there where we live with Granny, but I just don't take the time to notice or care. Here, with such beautiful grounds, bushes, hedges, flowers and a small fountain, I felt different, almost as if I was out of the city. I imagined it wasn't as big a deal for the others. They looked like they took it all for granted . . . big houses, birds, trees, flowers and fountains.

"I see your gardener took out those oleanders," Jade said, remembering what Doctor Marlowe had told us the day before.

"Yes. I hated to see them go, but they were dying and had to be replaced."

"My mother doesn't know one flower or bush from the other on our property. She only knows they cost a lot," Misty muttered. "She deliberately got a new gardener recently who's more expensive." She smiled and added, "Because it's part of the agreement she has with Daddy that he has to maintain the property. That was one wham-bam of an argument — the new gardener," she told us gleefully. She had a mischievous looking little smile on her face.

Sophie brought out a jug of lemonade and the pizzas. It occurred to me that if we weren't brought here by our parents, courts and schools, the chances of the four of us sitting around a table and having lunch together were almost as small as Granny winning the lottery. Maybe we had passed each other in some mall or in the lobby of some movie theater, but I was sure we had never looked at each other and actually seen each other. Up until now we were as good as invisible to each other.

"I wasn't sure if everyone liked pizza," Doctor Marlowe said as she took a seat. "It's just a good bet."

"I eat everything," Misty said.

It was something I would have expected Cat to say. She was the one who looked like she could afford to shed some pounds. However, when she ate, she ate like a mouse, nibbling with hesitation like she thought she was going to be caught doing something illegal.

"Of course, my mother thinks that's terrible," Misty continued. "She has this list of foods she pinned on the wall in the kitchen. She calls it her *Ten Most Wanted No-Nos* because they will wreak havoc on your complexion and make you fat. Pizza is at the top of the list," she said, and bit into her piece with added pleasure.

"Momma gave my brother Rodney leftover pizza for breakfast sometimes," I said.

"You're kidding. For breakfast? Did she at least give him a daily vitamin?" Misty asked.

I looked at her as if she was crazy.

"You look pretty good. What's your brother's health like?" Jade asked.

Doctor Marlowe sat back and ate her piece quietly with a tight smile on her lips. It made me feel like we were all being taped for some psychological study she was doing.

"Granny calls him a beanpole. He's almost as tall as I am already. He looks like my daddy more than he does Momma. He's a good boy, shy and quiet, too quiet for his teachers. He's not doing so good in school."

"Well," Jade corrected.

"What?"

"He's not doing so well in school."

"Yes, Miss Perfect," I said. "He's not doing so well. Maybe, if you got the time, you can come over and tutor my brother."

Cat stopped chewing and looked from Jade to me, anticipating more nasty words.

"I'm sorry," Jade said. "It's a habit, correcting people. When I do it to my mother, she gets all flustered. And maybe I will," she added.

"Will what?" Misty asked.

"Tutor her brother. I've done it in school as part of the Big Sister program."

"Sure," I said. "Only, I won't hold my breath."

"People do help each other sometimes," Jade said, "no matter what you think."

"Right," I said. "Look how much we're already helping each other."

She smirked. Maybe we couldn't be friends after all, I thought. Maybe we were what Granny called Momma and Daddy: Oil and Water.

"I hope you girls will eat all this. I don't want to have it in the house. It's too tempting," Doctor Marlowe said. She looked at Cat, who was encouraged to take a real bite.

"Where's Emma today?" Misty asked. I wondered if, like me, she was imagining Emma eating it all. Doctor Marlowe's sister was twice her width.

"She's a little under the weather. She has bad sinus trouble, especially on days like this," Doctor Marlowe explained.

"How long have you and Emma lived in this house?" Jade asked her.

"I've been here all my life. My situation after my parents divorced was a little different from your situations. My sister and I lived with my father because my mother wanted it that way."

"Why?" Misty asked first.

Cat looked up with interest, probably just as eager as the rest of us to know more about the person who was supposed to bring us to all the important answers about ourselves.

"My mother was more into her career than into being a wife and a mother. I suppose that contributed to why they got a divorce in the first place, not that I'm suggesting for one moment she couldn't or shouldn't have had a career."

"So you lived here with your father?" Jade asked.

"Yes, and then Emma returned about twenty-two years ago after her divorce," she said.

"So actually you've lived in the same house all your life?" Misty asked.

"Yes."

"What did your daddy do?" I asked. Since everyone else was badgering her with questions and she wasn't refusing to answer, I thought I might ask something too.

"He was a corporate attorney and my mother taught Drama-speech at UCLA," she revealed. "I saw her often, more often after I had gone to college."

"Are they both dead?" I asked.

"My father is," she said. "My mother is at an adult residency now. She suffers from Alzheimer's disease. You all know what that is?"

"You forget everything," Misty said.

"What a good idea," Jade quipped. Everyone stopped eating and looked at her. She shrugged. "If we could forget everything and then start over like a blank cassette, I mean."

"You don't have to forget the past," Doctor Marlowe said softly. "What you've got to learn to do is handle it, live with it, put it in perspective, keep it from permitting you to have a future.

"After all, that's what we're here to do," she concluded.

No one responded. We continued eating instead, each of us hoping she was right. Misty and Jade got into a conversation about clothes and Misty admitted she had some very nice things to wear when she wanted to, but just felt more comfortable in jeans and T-shirts.

From the way the others acted when Doctor Marlowe offered to show us the rest of the house when we finished eating, I gathered they, like me, were brought only to the office before this. She took us to the living room first and explained some of the paintings her father had purchased in Europe years and years ago. She told us he favored the Impressionists and one of the paintings was an authentic Monet. I didn't know anything much about Art, but I saw that Jade was impressed.

One picture caught all our interests. It was a painting of a little girl, maybe seven or eight, standing by a pond and looking at her own reflection in the water.

"My father liked this one a great deal, too," Doctor Marlowe said, standing behind us. "He told me that to him it was as if the little girl realized for the first time that she was really beautiful."

"That's not supposed to be the first time she'd seen herself, is it?" I asked.

"I don't think so, no."

"Maybe nobody told her she was pretty and so she thought she wasn't," Misty said.

"And she didn't dare hope otherwise," Jade added.

"Maybe they told her she wasn't pretty and she knew they were liars," Cat interjected with more anger in her voice than we had heard before. Misty shifted her eyes to look at her. Jade kept staring at the picture, but nudged me. I looked at Cat. She had her teeth clenched and her eyes looked like they had a little candle behind them.

"Does the painting have a name?" Misty asked.

"It's called *Reflections in a Pond*," Doctor Marlowe said.

"That's it?"

"Sometimes, things are nothing more than what they are," Doctor Marlowe replied.

"If that were the case all the time, you'd be out of work," Jade quipped.

Doctor Marlowe laughed hard. She really roared. It brought smiles to all our faces. I felt so light and happy that I almost didn't want to go back to the office and tell the rest of my story. I knew what that was going to do to our merry mood.

But that's what we had come here to do and anyway, everyone expected it. We all went to the bathroom and then settled back in the office.

"I really appreciate how smoothly things are going here. Thank you, girls," Doctor Marlowe said after we were seated. Then she turned to me.

Here I go again, I thought. It was like getting on a roller coaster.

"I keep saying things got worse after this and worse after that," I began, "so you probably all think it was about as bad as it could be, but it wasn't. It got worse again when Momma got a boyfriend.

"I knew she was going out with different men from time to time, but she never brought anyone home with her before Aaron Marks. He was someone new to the neighborhood and One-Eyed Bill's, which is where they met, of course.

"I gotta say that I never thought Momma was faithful to Daddy when they were together anyway. Whenever Daddy went off on a job that took a few days, I had the feeling Momma was with someone. She'd never admit it to me, of course, but you hear things on the street, hear talk and whatnot and just pick up on it if you wanted to be smart enough.

"Momma'd be with me and meet some girlfriend from One-Eyed Bill's and they'd get to talking and laughing and I could read between the lines that Momma went off with someone, maybe even just to his car behind the bar or something. I was worried she'd get some disease or get pregnant with some other man's baby, but I was afraid to say anything.

"If I looked suspicious or surprised, she'd just say, 'You know Shirley was fooling. She doesn't mean half of what she says, Star. Don't you go saying anything to your Daddy or Granny, hear?'

"If I didn't answer she'd slap me on the arm or shoulder until I turned to her and cried, 'What?'

" 'When I'm talking to you, I expect you to say something. You understand what I told you?'

" 'Yes,' I'd cry.

" 'Well, you just don't make any trouble for me. I got enough trouble without you making any,' she'd say and mumble the rest of the way home.

"I know it sounds like we never had any mother-daughter talks like you all probably have had with your mothers, but we did. Not toward the end, of course, but before things got so bad so that I couldn't look at her, much less talk to her."

I paused and turned to Misty.

"I remember yesterday how you kept asking how two people who were supposedly in love could suddenly hate each other so much. What happened to all the nice things they said to each other and the nice things they did together? I thought about that too and one day, when Momma was sober enough and being nice to Rodney, I asked her something like that.

"I said, 'You loved Daddy once, didn't you, Momma?'

" 'So?' she said.

" 'I was just wondering why you stopped, is all,' I said. I didn't want to spoil her good mood, so I spoke softly and looked down quickly.

" 'Because he's not the man I fell in love with,' she said. 'He fooled me is what happened. When we were first going together, he used to tell me how different he was and how different things were going to be for us. We're not going to be like these poor, drifting folks around us. We're going to build a real home.

" 'He was going to have his own company and I'd be a lady in style. I'd have my own car and we'd have a nice house and on and on he'd go with that web he was spinning to trap me good. That's what he did. I gave myself to him expecting he'd live up to those promises. Every one of them turned out to be just a lot of hot air and when I asked him what happened to all those promises, he said he's doing the best he could, to be patient.

" ' "Be patient? I'm growing old being patient," I told him. Then he'd clam up the way he often did and pretend I wasn't in the room. He could be so infuriating. You know that. You've seen him like that.'

" 'Maybe he was trying,' I risked saying. She

didn't get mad. She laughed.

" 'Yeah. Look around you at the palace he built. Men,' she said, 'are born liars. Don't believe a one.'

"She looked down at Rodney playing with his toy truck on the floor and shook her head.

" 'They're so sweet when they're little boys and then something happens to them. They let their thing take over and run their lives and ruin ours,' she said.

"I knew what she was saying, but I just didn't believe she was saying it. Momma and I never really had a heart to heart about sex and stuff. She just assumed I'd learn it like she did, from girlfriends. I guess when your hormones screamed, it was all supposed to just pop into your head and you'd know what to do and what not to do. Most girls didn't know what not," I said. "At least, most I knew."

"My mother didn't exactly offer me any sage advice," Jade said.

"Excuse me?"

"Womanly wisdom," she muttered with that cork-screw smirk of hers.

"Oh. We got taught stuff by the school nurse, of course. She even gave girls sanitary napkins. I remember when I first started getting cramps, I complained to Momma and she just handed me one and told me to wear it just in case.

" 'In case?' I asked her.

" 'Well, look at you,' Momma declared, 'you about to bust out, aren't you? Welcome to woman's misery.'

"That was about all she told me about it. I learned the rest from girlfriends and the nurse's pamphlets. Then one day when I was nearly thirteen it just happened. It was like an explosion inside me. I got this terrible cramp which about folded me over. I couldn't move without the pain. The nurse came down to the classroom to help me back to her office. I saw the other girls laughing behind my back and some of the boys, too, but I was suffering too much to care.

"She had me rest and called home. Momma answered and after the nurse told her about me, Momma said, 'Well, what am I supposed to do about it?'

"The nurse told her she should come for me, but she claimed she couldn't because Rodney was home sick, which I had a feeling was a big fat lie. She was probably with someone and drinking. When I was able to get up and about, I went home myself and discovered I was right.

"That was the first time I met Aaron Marks. The music was loud. They had been drinking gin. Momma was wearing only a slip. When Momma saw I had entered, she stopped dancing with Aaron and wobbled for a moment and then laughed.

" 'This here's my daughter, Star. She started the monthlies today.' She lifted a glass full of gin and added, 'Let's toast to her happy days.'

"I didn't take much of a look at Aaron Marks that first time. I was so embarrassed, I just made a dash for my bedroom and slammed the door. I heard them laughing and drinking. When Rodney came home, they were in Momma's bedroom. I hurried out and brought him into my room and told him to just stay there. He cried because he had to go to the bathroom so I had to let him out and he heard Momma's laughter and went to her room. The sight of another man in bed with her just put the freeze in his face.

"Rodney ain't only shy. When he gets frightened or upset, he has a hard time talking and starts to stutter. It almost sounds like he's choking on a chicken bone. I grabbed his hand and pulled him back to my room. He sat staring with his eyes full of questions I couldn't even begin to answer for him.

" 'She's drinking again,' I told him. 'We have to wait here until it's over.'

"It was like hiding in a storm basement while a hurricane or tornado passed overhead. I tried to keep him occupied, but every time we heard a laugh or something bang against the wall or on the floor, we both froze and listened, our hearts pounding. I knew Rodney was afraid of the new man in her naked arms, but I didn't know anything more about Aaron Marks than Rodney did at the time.

"I prayed that it would all end soon, but it went on and on that whole afternoon, until Momma passed out and Aaron quietly left the apartment. I heard the front door open and close and then I inched out of my room, leaving Rodney behind. I looked in on Momma. She was naked, facedown on her bed, snoring away.

"Maybe all that made my first period worse. I don't know. I hear that stress and such can make trouble for you in that way."

I gazed at Doctor Marlowe, who nodded slightly.

"I had such bad cramps, I could barely move about the kitchen to make Rodney something for dinner. I finally gave up and just made him a peanut butter sandwich. He was still too scared to eat much anyway.

"He fell asleep on my bed that night and I let him stay even though I had a very bad night and had to get up and change and just walked about moaning and groaning. Some time very late, I heard Momma get up and bang into a chair in the kitchen. I heard her curse and run the water and then she went back to sleep and was still sleeping in the morning. She woke up as I helped Rodney get ready for another day of school.

"I felt like I had been punched and punched in the stomach. I ached right down the back of my legs and I was in a nasty mood myself, so when Momma stuck her head out to ask what was going on, I shouted back at her.

" 'What do you think is going on? It's morning and Rodney slept in my room all night because of your carrying on with that man,' I cried.

"She blinked as if she couldn't remember if she had or not and then she got mad at me for yelling at her and started screaming back.

" 'I ain't got rid of that man you called your daddy just to have you on my back,' she said. 'Don't you go lecturing to me, hear? You don't open your mouth.'

" 'Yeah, well you should learn to keep yours closed,' I snapped back and she looked like her eyes exploded in her head. She came charging across the kitchen to slap me, only I wasn't going to let her slap me anymore. I had been in enough pain all the previous afternoon and night anyway so I pushed a chair in her path and she fell right over it. It stunned her and she just lay there staring up at the ceiling.

"Rodney was in a terrible state. He wasn't just stuttering and frozen now. He was trembling so much that I heard his teeth click. I pushed him up and out of the apartment, taking his hand and walking him out of the building. I forgot everything: my books, my purse, everything, including the sanitary napkins, of course."

"Oh no," Misty groaned.

"Yeah," I said. "I had an accident after I brought him to his school."

"What did you do?" Cat asked. She was leaning toward me now, her hands clasped on her lap.

"I wanted to go to Granny's but I didn't have any money for the bus, so I had no choice. I had to make my way home. I practically snuck back into the apartment. Momma was back in bed with a cold rag over her forehead. She didn't hear me. I tiptoed around, got what I needed,

74

changed, and then slipped out of the apartment. I was late to school and they sent me to the assistant principal, Mr. McDermott, who wanted to put me in detention because I had a record of tardiness that stretched from one side of his office to the other. That's what he told me.

"I told him I couldn't stay. I had to be home for my little brother. He said if I didn't, I'd be in bigger trouble and he told me that my mother would just have to take care of my little brother. That's when I guess I went a little nuts. That was the first time."

I paused. Even though I had eaten plenty at lunch, I suddenly had this terribly empty feeling in my stomach made worse by the sensation of a fistful of worms crawling around in there. I squirmed, took a breath and closed my eyes. I felt dizzy and had to lay back.

"Let's all give Star a couple of minutes," Doctor Marlowe said. "I meant to show you all my library," she added. "Star, take a little break," she added. "Lie down for a moment if you like."

I did and I heard them all leave.

"She'll be fine," I heard Doctor Marlowe tell them just outside of the office. Their footsteps died away.

Whenever I recalled Momma falling over that chair and hitting the floor, I remember the way Rodney's mouth opened wide, but nothing came out. Where did that scream go? I wondered. If you swallow back a scream, does it echo in your heart? There is something extra terrifying about seeing your mother or your father faint, fall, get hurt. They're your parents and in your mind, as silly as it may be, you think they are like Superman and Superwoman. Nothing happens to parents. Parents are there to take care of us. We get sick. We fall and scrape our knees. We burn ourselves and do silly and stupid things, but they are always there to comfort and look after us. We're too young and frightened to take care of them. Nothing happens to them.

Momma didn't have an iota of dignity when she flopped over that chair. She flailed about like a fish out of water for a few moments and groaned. As I hurried Rodney out, I looked back at her and saw her dazed expression. She didn't know why she was on the floor. It had surprised and frightened her more than it had hurt her.

The tears were streaming down Rodney's face so fast, I couldn't wipe them off. As soon as the ones on his cheeks were gone, they were followed by more until I held him tightly and promised him things would be all right.

"I'll go back and help her," I promised. "You just go to school and everything will be all right later. You'll see."

He stopped trembling and after we walked some more, he calmed down enough to at least go to school. But the memory of all that was too much for me to swallow. It came up and up like bad food and I had this rush of dizziness and the trembles.

It passed after a few calm moments and I felt

my breathing get regular again. I sat up, drank some water and went to the window. The rain had stopped. Sunlight was slicing through the clouds, turning the drops into jewels on the leaves and on the grass. Everything glittered and looked fresh and clean.

It really wasn't much of a storm, I thought, but it was something, and now look how beautiful the world becomes.

Why can't that be the same for us?

Why can't Doctor Marlowe help us spread the dark clouds apart and let in some sunshine?

I heard them coming back and sucked in my breath, willing to try, willing to hope.

That was something, at least.

Wasn't it?

4

"How are you doing?" Doctor Marlowe asked as soon as they were all back in the office.

"I'm okay," I said.

"We can stop for today," she suggested.

I saw the looks of concern on the other girls' faces. They looked sincere, worried.

"I'm all right," I said more firmly. "I'd rather get it all out and finished than have to sleep on it and come back and do it again tomorrow."

Doctor Marlowe looked at the girls and they all took their seats. I remained standing, my arms folded under my breasts. I felt like one of those lawyers on television talking to a jury. Doctor Marlowe was the judge and the other girls were the jury, but who did I want to make look guilty? Just my parents or the whole world?

"Doctor Marlowe always says we should try to face our demons head on," I said.

Jade nodded. Misty's lips relaxed into a small smile and Cat stared intensely, making me think hard about every single word.

"I hate remembering that day, but I hate being afraid of the memory more. Anyway, after the assistant principal threatened me again, I just started screaming and pounding my own legs. It felt good, like I was unloading all this weight. I guess he'd never seen anything like it and went rushing out for the nurse. She came back with him. By that time, I was pulling on my hair and shaking my head so hard, I could feel my neck twisting to the point of snapping. The nurse put her arm around me and tried to hold me.

" 'Call for the paramedics!' she ordered and the assistant principal ran out again to do it. I did calm down, but I couldn't stop gasping. I had painful hiccups too. The paramedics came in and got me to lay down on the stretcher. They buckled me in and rolled me out of the office and put me in the ambulance.

"There were lots of kids watching from windows and from the doorway, but I didn't care.

"At the hospital emergency room, they lifted me onto a table in an examination room and left me there. A nurse looked in on me from time to time and kept telling me the doctor would come soon, but I think I was there for almost an hour before any doctor showed up. I kept dozing off and waking to the sounds in the hallway: people crying, orders being shouted, footsteps and stretchers being rolled.

"They called Momma but she didn't answer. She had gone out, I guess. That's what she told everyone later anyway. The nurse came in to ask me if I knew where she might be and I told her about One-Eyed Bill's.

"Finally, the doctor saw me. I was asleep when he came and he woke me up and told me I'd be fine and I didn't even need any medicines. I remember thinking he was very young, too young to be a real doctor.

" 'What I believe you experienced was an anxiety attack,' he said. 'You've got some heavy personal problems,' he added.

"He recommended I see the hospital psychologist. When Momma finally showed up, he told her the same thing and wrote out the name of the doctor.

"She was angry more than worried because it cost her two cab fares, one to come down to get me and then one to get me back home. From what I could tell, she couldn't remember what had happened that morning. She told the young doctor I'd be all right and I didn't need to see a psychologist and besides, there was no money for such things. We didn't have health isurance.

"So I went home with her and went to bed. She gave Rodney dinner and then I woke up because she was moving Rodney's cot-bed and things into my room. She pretended she was doing it for me, but I would soon learn she was doing it because she wanted to bring Aaron Marks home with her and Aaron didn't want a child in the same room.

"Momma then went off to work at One-Eyed

Bill's as if nothing had happened. Rodney didn't understand why I had been in a hospital, but he was happy to be in my room, staying as close to me as he could. I was so tired from my period and the events, I couldn't keep my eyes open. I remember I helped him go to sleep and then I slept so deeply, I thought I dreamed hearing Momma come home, hearing her laughter and Aaron's voice. It was real late.

"I woke before Rodney did the next morning and I sat up thinking about my dreams, wondering how much was true and how much was imagined. A little afraid and a little curious, I slipped off the bed and walked barefoot to the door of Momma's bedroom. It was shut tight, but I opened it slowly and quietly and peeked in to find Aaron Marks beside her in the bed, the both of them naked, their arms twisted around each other like pipe cleaners.

"I closed the door and quickly retreated to my bedroom, still feeling too sick to have an appetite or to want to get up and dress.

"Rodney got himself up and all, but he didn't want to go to school. I had to force him. I wanted him out of the house so he wouldn't see Aaron there. I stayed in my room until I heard Aaron get up and go.

"The school nurse called and I told her I was fine and resting. Momma still hadn't gotten up. When I went out to the kitchen though, she shouted for me to make her some coffee and bring it to her.

" 'As long as you're home, you might as well be of some use,' she said.

"I made her the coffee and brought it to her. She groaned and sat up, keeping her eyes closed as if the lids had been turned to lead. After a sip, she fluttered them open. They were so blood-shot, I could barely make out the pupils.

" 'Your brother off to school?' she asked. Why didn't she think of that first? I thought.

" 'Yes. That man was here with you last night,' I said.

" 'So? Get used to it. I ain't becoming a nun just because your no-good-for-nothing of a father deserted me. Truth is, he wasn't much of a lover-man anyway.'

"I didn't want to hear any more of it so I went back to my room. She spent almost the whole morning sleeping and then she went to work earlier, probably to meet up with Aaron, I thought. As usual, I made Rodney supper and helped him with his schoolwork. By now we were almost by ourselves in the world anyway.

"When I returned to school the next day, the assistant principal didn't bother me. Most of the other kids had found out about my episode in his office and there was gossip, but after a while, they lost interest in it and for me it was just like a bad dream.

"This particular episode had all begun with my first period. That was my entrance to wom-anhood," I added. "For a while after, every time I got my period, I thought about all those events.

Maybe remembering made it worse for me each time. Things certainly didn't get any easier around the house and Aaron was there more than I wanted him to be. The more Momma did with him, the less she did for Rodney and me, not that she ever did all that much.

"There were times when we didn't have what to eat and I had to go look for her to get some money. She tried having a charge account at the Spanish grocery on the block, but when she failed to pay the bill on time twice, they stopped letting us charge things. Rodney was eating so much peanut butter, he could have made commercials for the company.

"He was outgrowing shoes and clothes, but Momma didn't seem to notice or care unless I pointed it out and then there was all the complaining about how much things cost and where was my good-for-nothing father who could make a kid but not care for him? If Momma was drunk, she could rant about this for hours. I'd hear her voice in my dreams. I used to think her shouting and hollering got stuck on the walls like glue and just played itself over and over until I was sleeping with my hands over my ears or my pillow over my head.

"It's raining pain, I would tell myself. Once, when Momma began one of her frequent tirades, I actually went to the closet, took out the umbrella and opened it, holding it between me and her. She went wild, screaming about all the bad luck I was bringing into the house.

" 'What about all you're bringing in?' I screamed back and she threw a frying pan at me. It would have hit me if I didn't have the umbrella and use it like a shield.

"Rodney started to cry so I scooped him up and went to my room, shutting the door. She kept yelling for a while and then settled down, but while she did, I held Rodney and petted his hair and kept him from crying. It got harder and harder for me to handle it all until one day, I did something that helped, something that really could stop the rain of pain."

"I'd like to hear about that," Jade said. "Nothing really helps me."

"Me too," Cat added softly, almost under her breath. "What stopped your pain?"

Misty just had that happy-go-lucky smile on her face as if she knew.

"I had a blanket when I was little that Daddy once jokingly called my magic carpet. It stuck in my head and when I saw the movie *Aladdin* and saw the magic carpet, it made a big impression on me."

"So you went flying off on your blanket?" Jade asked with disappointment darkening her eyes.

"I suppose I did," I said.

"What?" Misty said, her smile widening. She looked at Jade, who grimaced, shook her head and raised her eyes toward the ceiling.

"Go on and laugh, but it worked for me."

"What worked for you?" Jade demanded. "You're not making any sense."

"I took my blanket and put it on my bed and lay down on it, folded myself up so my knees almost touched my stomach. It felt better that way."

"Oh," Jade said as if she thought that was it: a way to ease the menstrual cramps.

"And then I left," I added.

"Left?"

"Yeah, I guess I left in my imagination, but it helped. I saw myself flying off, out the window and out the city. I went to every place I ever dreamed about or saw on television and wished I was.

"I floated over the ocean, over forests and other cities. I actually saw things as if I was up high, everything looking so small like toys. My imaginary trips took long too because when I returned to my bed, more than an hour passed sometimes and I always felt better.

"It got so I began to lay on my blanket whenever I was unhappy or Momma made me mad. I'd just wander off to my room, spread the blanket out on the bed and spread myself over it, folding my legs and closing my eyes. Then I was gone and I didn't hear anything, not Momma's stream of complaints or drunken laughter or shouts at Rodney. I was gone.

"When I came back, I felt refreshed, lighter. Rodney would tell me he had shaken me to tell me something and I didn't open my eyes. He said he shook me hard and finally, he gave up. Once, he did it and just sat on the floor waiting and when I opened my eyes, he said he had been watching my face and I had been smiling so much. He wanted to know why. I didn't want to tell him so I just said I had had a good dream."

"That's all it was anyway, right?" Jade asked, looking to Doctor Marlowe, "a dream? She didn't go anywhere."

Doctor Marlowe hesitated before responding and looked at me as if she was deciding whether or not to bust my bubble.

"It might have been more than just a dream," she said. "It might be a form of meditation. I meditate myself," she confessed.

"I really don't know what that is," Misty said. "I thought it was the same as dreaming."

"No. When you dream you are really still in a conscious state but the mind is being bombarded by different images you don't control. Dreams are more or less random. You can deliberately think of things, but there's no guarantee you'll dream about them after you've fallen asleep. Meditation is a higher form. In meditation, you deliberately set out to put your mind on another plane, another level. What Star was doing was concentrating so hard on her desire to leave her surroundings, she took herself to a higher plane and the result was it relaxed her. People meditate to avoid stress."

"Can we do that, too?" Jade asked.

"Yes. After we've all had an opportunity to talk, we'll discuss ways to relieve the tension and stress you're all experiencing and one of those techniques will involve some meditation. I'm not suggesting it's the cure-all, but it can help."

"I always did feel better," I emphasized. The others looked at me with envy. "Sometimes, I wished I never came back," I said.

Doctor Marlowe's face grew darker, her eyes more intensely on me.

"There's always that danger," she said. "We're here to make sure that doesn't happen." She looked at the others. "To any of you."

Maybe it was the way she said it or the way the others looked after she had said it, but suddenly it occurred to me how serious all this was, how we were all walking along the edge of different cliffs and how we could misstep and fall or deliberately fall into our own private oblivion. The atmosphere in Doctor Marlowe's office suddenly seemed heavier, all of us lost for a moment or two, thinking about our personal danger. I didn't know Jade's story or Cat's yet, but I looked from face to face and saw an identical terror in their eyes. I saw the concern in Doctor Marlowe's too and I remembered what Granny had said when she had dropped me off this morning.

"You're too young to become someone's lost cause, hear?"

I hear, Granny, I thought. I hear.

They were all waiting for me to continue. I took a breath and did so.

"I was listening closely to you yesterday, Misty, when you started talking about how you felt about your father's girlfriend and about going to his apartment when you knew she was there with him and what it was like for you," I said. "But at least you could choose to go or not.

"I was about fifteen by now. One afternoon when I came home from school with Rodney, we saw suitcases and a couple of boxes in Momma's room. She wasn't there. Rodney looked at me and I thought first, maybe it's Daddy. Maybe he's finally come back.

"Rodney couldn't remember him, but I could, of course. Lots of times I have come here and talked about how I felt about my daddy, so I guess I should talk a little more about him. I told you how I was always hoping that he would return and how I always hoped the phone was ringing because he was on the other end ready to tell Momma he was on his way.

"We all talked about hate here, maybe me more than anyone yet. Maybe Jade and Cat are going to say a lot more when their turn comes, but my granny isn't wrong when she says hate is a two-edged sword. Yeah, you stick it in someone, but you're sticking it in yourself at the same time. That's what the minister said in church one Sunday when I went with Granny. She kept shifting her eyes at me as he preached about driving the hate out of your heart before it rots the good in you.

"Nothing made me hate my daddy more than his leaving us, and nothing made me want him more. When I was little and we had some good times, I remember him carrying me on his shoulders. I remember holding onto his hand, feeling how tight and strong a grip he had, and I remember never being afraid as long as he was with us.

"After he left and me and Momma and Rodney went anywhere, I couldn't help but feel this empty place beside us. Sometimes, I'd forget and think Daddy just walked away for a moment. He will be standing right next to me soon. Of course, he wouldn't, but that didn't stop me from glancing to the side and thinking about him.

"Momma's a tough little woman. I don't think too many people, including men, would want to tangle with her. She could be a wildcat, so it wasn't that I was physically afraid. I just felt . . . like we were less, if that makes any sense," I said.

Misty looked like she understood more than the other two. Jade turned her eyes from me and Cat stared at the floor.

"What I mean is it didn't help me just to have another man come into our house. It didn't make me feel better or safer. If anything, I think it went the other way.

"But that's what those boxes and suitcases meant: Aaron Marks was moving in to live with Momma. I could smell him in the room already.

" 'Whose is that?' Rodney wanted to know. 'Are we moving away, Star? Did Momma pack us up?'

" 'No Rodney. We aren't moving anywhere. We're stuck here.'

"About two hours later, the door opened. Momma and Aaron came in, both laughing. I was mashing up some potatoes for Rodney to have with his hamburger. Momma was dressed in her Sunday clothes and Aaron was in a suit with the tie loose. He was not quite as tall as my daddy and much wider in the hips with a little paunch. His head was rounder and his hair was thinner, showing a lot more forehead, which I thought made his eyes look larger. He had a nose with a bump in it because it had been broken a few times. He had tried to be a prizefighter when he was younger and ended up being one of those sparring partners that gets his head beat in regularly, which was what I thought accounted for his dull, dumb face and empty eyes.

"As you can tell, I was never fond of Aaron. I never could understand what Momma saw in him and when I said so once, she just laughed and said, 'When you start being with a man, you'll understand what matters most about him.'

"I wasn't stupid. I understood she meant sex.

"Anyway, I stood there, gazing at the two of them, both wearing these big fat grins that put little drops of ice down my back and around my heart. I reached out and pulled Rodney closer to me and he held onto my leg.

" 'Well, there she is, my little cook,' Momma cried. 'Or our little cook.'

" 'What are you talking about, Momma? What's going on?'

"Aaron laughed and went to the cabinet below

90

the sink where Momma stored her vodka, gin and bourbon. He took out the bourbon and said it was time for another celebration.

" 'Right you are about that,' Momma cried.

"I watched him pour them each half a glass of bourbon and then toast and drink. Rodney didn't fully understand what booze was, but he hated the smell and the taste and just knew that whenever Momma drank some, she was usually unpleasant and often frightening, so he clung tighter to me.

" 'Why are you celebrating, Momma?' I finally asked.

"The two of them looked at each other and laughed as if I had asked the silliest question.

" 'Momma?'

" ' 'Cause Aaron and I just got married,' she said.

"Naturally, I grimaced and shook my head.

" 'You can't marry Aaron, Momma. You're already married,' I told her.

"The smile flew off her face like a frightened sparrow and she slammed her glass down on the counter so hard, it almost shattered.

" 'A man just walks out of here one day and never calls,' she said pointing at the door, 'never comes back, never sends a note, and goes off with another woman and I'm still supposed to be married to him? No ma'am, I'm not.'

" 'Don't you have to go to a court, though?' I asked.

" 'Courts mean lawyers and lawyers are just

crooks who hang out a shingle off their doors,' she said. 'Aaron and I talked it over and I declared, officially declared that is,' she added pulling up her shoulders and standing as straight as she could, 'that I ain't married to Kenny Fisher no more. I declared it this afternoon and then we went over to Preacher Longstreet down in South Central and he married us right and proper with a Bible and all. I even got a ring,' she bragged and stuck out her hand. It didn't look like much of a ring, but I didn't say so.

" 'Don't you have to get a license and stuff?' I asked.

" 'Will you stop with all those questions. Just say hello to your new daddy,' she ordered.

"I turned back to the potatoes.

" 'Star, you hear me? You show your new daddy respect, hear?'

" 'He's not my daddy,' I said.

" 'What? What did you say?'

"She started for me, but Aaron held her back.

" 'Hold on now, Aretha,' he said. 'We don't want any unpleasantries tonight on our wedding night. Our honeymoon,' he added and she stopped fighting him and smiled.

" 'You're right, Aaron.' She looked at me, her eyes shooting darts across the kitchen. 'We'll talk about this later. Aaron and I are going out for a celebration dinner. I just want to freshen up a bit,' she said and went to the bathroom.

"I continued to work on Rodney's dinner and he held onto me the whole time. It was difficult to breathe, not to be drowned by everything that was happening so fast.

" 'That boy looks like a sissy holding onto you like that,' Aaron said. A terrible anger washed over me. I felt the heat rise into my face.

"I turned and glared at him, gave him my coldest look and said, 'He'll grow up to be easily twice the man you are, not that it would be hard to do.'

"He stared at me for a moment and I saw rage start to build in his eyes, but suddenly he stopped it as if he knew he might lose control of himself if he didn't. He laughed, but it was one of those soft, unsure laughs, a laugh to cover up his own discomfort.

"I didn't stop glaring at him and he pointed his thick, crooked right forefinger at me.

" 'Your momma's right about you. You're too sassy. We'll deal with it later,' he said and went to the bedroom to start unpacking and moving in."

I paused and looked at the other girls. Each in her eyes showed she understood what a low moment that was for me and my little brother. I didn't even have to ask, but I did.

"How would you like that to happen to you?"

Doctor Marlowe's face brightened with interest and excitement as she looked at them and waited.

"They make decisions about our lives as if we were nothing more than ornaments on Christmas trees," Jade said, her eyes darkening as she fixed on her own thoughts.

"My daddy never even told me he was seeing someone else, much less look for my opinion about it," Misty said.

Cat remained quiet, but her eyes filled with a cold look of fear that made me wonder again how different her life had been and what troubles she had seen, troubles so bad they had stolen her voice and her smile.

"Yeah, well despite what Aaron and Momma threatened, Momma didn't say anything more about it to me that night. She and Aaron went to their celebration and came home very late. Their door was closed when I got up the next morning. Rodney and I had our breakfast and left without seeing them, which was fine with me.

"Aaron supposedly worked for a used-car dealer, but I always thought he did something else on the side, something illegal. After he moved in, there were lots of phone calls for him at all hours of the night, and he would always talk too low for me to hear.

"Right from the start, I was never comfortable with him in the house and especially uncomfortable when he was there without Momma. Most of the time, he was out or with Momma at One-Eyed Bill's, but when he wasn't, he made both me and Rodney nervous and Rodney would just retreat from the living room and stay in our bedroom. It wasn't a big apartment, probably not much bigger than this office, and we had only one bathroom for all of us to share.

"But I want to say right away that he never

tried anything with me. I know that's the first thing everyone's supposed to think, but he didn't and he had his reasons, which he came out and told me once."

"I'd like to hear about that," Jade said.

"I thought you might."

"What's that supposed to mean?" she fired back.

We stared at each other for a moment and then she smiled and I just laughed and shook my head. Cat's eyes filled with confusion and she looked at Misty.

"Maybe after dealing with us you oughta re-think the use of the word *crazy*, Doctor Marlowe," she said.

Doctor Marlowe laughed.

"The only place I approve of its use is in the Patsy Cline song," she said.

"Who's Patsy Cline?" Misty asked and looked from me to Jade.

"She's a country singer, or was, right?" Jade asked Doctor Marlowe.

"Yes."

"Oh."

"There is other music besides hip-hop and rock, girls."

"I know who she is," Cat said. "My father listened to her music, but my mother threw all of his stuff out of the house after he was gone, just like Misty's mother did, except my mother even got rid of the bedsheets, blankets and pillow-cases he had used."

No one spoke. We could hear footsteps in the hallway, a door close and then the sound of a vacuum cleaner Sophie had started.

"So, are we going to hear more about Aaron Marks or not?" Jade asked impatiently.

"He's not that interesting to hear about," I said, "but yeah, I'll tell you more about Aaron.

"I'll tell you more about it all."

5

"Early one evening about two months later, I gave Rodney dinner and then decided to take a bath. I had my portable CD going with my earphones on and I didn't hear Aaron come home. He rushed into the apartment and moments later, he was in the bathroom."

"Didn't you lock the door?" Jade asked.

"The lock was broken some time ago and nobody bothered to fix it," I said.

I was about to continue when I looked up at her, and I noticed Cat was twisting her left hand so hard, I couldn't imagine it not hurting her. I studied her and noticed her legs begin to tremble. Her knees were practically knocking together.

I glanced at Doctor Marlowe, who was studying Cat even harder than I was. She leaned over and took Cathy's right hand to stop her from twisting her left. Cat's legs slowed their trembling.

"It's all right, Cathy," Doctor Marlowe nearly whispered. "We're listening to Star now."

Cathy looked up at her and a calm seemed to settle in those frantic eyes.

"Okay?" Doctor Marlowe asked.

Cat nodded. Doctor Marlowe smiled, patted her hand and sat back.

"Sorry," she said. I still hesitated. "Everyone's fine, Star. Go on."

"It's not that bad so nobody's got to go get worked up or nothing," I muttered.

"We'll be the judge of that," Jade said. "What you think is bad and what I think is bad might not be the same thing."

"Well, who says you're right?"

"Nobody says I'm right. It just might not be the same, that's all. You don't have to jump down my throat every time I open my mouth," she whined.

"Well, then don't say you'll be judging me. I don't need you to judge me."

"I didn't mean that literally. If you weren't so trigger-happy . . ."

"Girls," Doctor Marlowe warned before I could respond. She flashed a "no" at me.

I sat back, holding my eyes on Jade a moment longer. She turned away and crossed one leg over the other.

"I saw the bathroom door open and I screamed when Aaron came in. He acted as if I wasn't even there. He went to the sink, opened the cabinet and found his razor and shaving

98

cream. Really feeling sick, I still managed to find a voice.

" 'Get out of here!' I cried pulling off the earphones. 'I'm taking a bath.'

" 'Got to shave fast,' he muttered, looking at his ugly face in the mirror. 'I have to meet your mother in ten minutes. We got tickets to the heavyweight exhibition fight, but we can't be late or we'll lose the seats and they're great seats.'

" 'I don't care. I'm taking a bath. Get out!' I screamed now, covering myself the best I could.

"He looked down at me.

" 'I won't be but a few minutes and I ain't interested in you so don't worry,' he said. 'I don't touch virgins,' he bragged."

"What?" Jade said, coming back to life and turning to me. "He said he won't touch virgins?"

"That's what he said. He started to shave and kept talking, telling me that virgins were too much trouble and he preferred a woman who was broken in like a good riding horse. He laughed at his own joke.

"Meanwhile, I nearly shriveled to nothing in the water, of course, but he didn't look at me. He was more interested in himself. He finished shaving and rushed out again.

"My heart was pounding and I was furious. After he put on his suit and tie, he came hurrying back just after I had gotten out of the tub. I had the towel wrapped around me, but before I could protest, he grabbed his hairbrush, swiped himself a few times, and then turned and asked me, had the nerve to ask me, how he looked.

" 'Like a moron!' I screamed at him.

"He stood there, chewing his lip for a moment, nodded and then walked out of the apartment. That night I fixed the lock, even though it wasn't strong enough to hold him back if he ever wanted to come in."

"Did you tell your mother what happened?" Misty asked.

"No. She didn't get home until very late and even if I got up to talk to her, she wouldn't have been in any sort of condition to listen or care.

"Besides, what was I going to complain about? She would only have defended him for having to hurry and she'd say I was lollygagging in the tub or something. She'd defend him no matter what. I sensed that from the start."

"I always thought most mothers would defend their children no matter what," Misty muttered.

Jade snorted and Cathy shook her head.

"Not no matter what," Cathy said in a voice just a shade above a whisper.

"Momma never wanted us and she never made a big secret of it," I said.

"What was your grandmother doing all this time you were living with that monster in your house?" Jade asked, not hiding her anger.

"She wouldn't have hesitated to come over and get me and Rodney if I told her all the grimy details," I said, "but I couldn't for a long time."

"Why not?" Misty asked.

"About a month before Aaron moved in with

us, Granny had a heart attack," I said. It brought tears to my eyes just to mention it. "I didn't even know it had happened for two days afterward. Momma had kept it to herself. She probably knew I'd want to get down to the hospital right away and she didn't want to deal with it. She actually went to work the night they took Granny into the hospital. I found that out later, too.

"One of Granny's friends, Mary Wiggins, luckily had come to visit with her just minutes after Granny lost her breath and sat herself down on the floor in front of the sofa in her living room. That's the way Mary found her, clutching her breast, her eyes closed, gasping.

"She had the sense to call nine-one-one immediately and then tried to keep Granny calm. Granny was calm, even though she was struggling to breathe. I never saw anyone as calm about her own possible death as Granny. She has this abiding faith in the hereafter."

"What about you?" Misty asked. She looked at me like my answer really would matter to her.

"I always thought that if things were going to be good afterward, why couldn't they be good now? No one's looking after me in this world, why should I expect anyone will be in the next?" I told her. She nodded slowly, thinking. "We'll probably be on our own just as much," I added.

"My mother says this whole life is just a test," Cat offered.

"Yeah, well, I'd just as soon cheat and pass then," I said.

Jade laughed and Misty folded her face into a small smile, like someone half in and half out of a dream.

"Anyway, the way I found out about Granny was the hospital called for Momma while she was working. Granny wanted some things from her apartment and had asked the nurse to contact Momma. I felt real stupid not knowing she was in the hospital, stupid and angry.

"As soon as I hung up the phone, I searched through the dresser drawers in Momma's bedroom until I found where she hid some money. It was suppertime, but I grabbed Rodney's hand and dragged him out with me to the waiting taxicab that took us to the hospital. When we got there, I bought Rodney a candy bar to keep him satisfied while I went up to what they call the CCU and asked for Mrs. Patton. I thought they might not let me in, but when the nurse heard I was her granddaughter, she said it was okay. She said, 'It's about time someone came to visit her.'

"I started to cry and told her I had just learned my granny was there. My mother hadn't told me. The nurse softened her disapproving look and took me to Granny's bedside. She said Granny was doing very well, that the doctors decided there wasn't very much damage to her heart muscle, but she would have what they called angina pain from time to time. It was treatable, she said. I guess she was happy to finally have someone to talk to about Granny, someone who cared and would listen.

"Granny was surprised but happy to see me. I told her how Momma hadn't said a word and she just pressed her lips together and shook her head.

" 'It's okay. She probably didn't want you worrying,' Granny told me.

"She could forgive Judas," I said.

"Who?" Misty asked.

"Judas. You know, the one who betrayed Jesus."

"Oh."

"I guess you never went to Sunday school."

"Hardly," she said laughing. "The only prayers I ever heard in my house were, 'God, please don't let that be a gray hair.'

Jade really laughed and Cat widened her eyes and stretched her mouth in glee.

"Anyway, I stayed with her as long as I could and then I took Rodney to the hospital cafeteria and bought him and me some sandwiches with some of the money I had found in Momma's dresser drawer. Then I did to her what she had done to me."

"What was that?" Jade asked quickly.

"I didn't tell her anything. I got a cab home and Rodney and I did some schoolwork, watched some television and went to bed. I heard Momma come home at night, but I didn't go out to talk to her. In the morning, she was sleeping when Rodney and I got up. I fixed his breakfast and after we both got ready for school,

I left without telling her a thing about my hospital visit.

"She was home when we got back from school, but I never mentioned anything then either. I could tell she hadn't called the hospital because Granny would surely have said something about my visiting her.

"Momma didn't find out until the day after that when she finally checked on Granny, who I knew had been moved out of the CCU and into a room for a few more days of observation. I came home with Rodney and Momma was confused almost as much as she was upset. It was like she couldn't understand what had happened. Had she told me or hadn't she? I could see the uncertainty in her eyes.

" 'Why didn't you tell me you saw Granny in the hospital?' she demanded. 'You made me look like a fool.'

" 'You don't need me to do that. You do it yourself,' I said and she slapped me.

" 'Don't you talk back to me like that!' she screamed.

" 'Why didn't you tell me about Granny?' I wailed through my tears. 'The nurses thought nobody cared about her. You didn't even call to see how she was doing.'

" 'It's none of their damn business. Everybody sticks their nose in my life. I didn't tell you 'cause I knew you'd go off on me and carry on and make things harder.'

"She paused, thinking for a moment.

" 'How did you get there and back?' she asked. 'Where'd you get the money for carfare?'

"I didn't answer and she went stomping into her room and searched her drawer.

" 'You stole from me!' she screamed. 'You went and took my rainy day stash.'

" 'That wasn't there for a rainy day, Momma,' I said. 'It's been raining around here for some time and you never touch it until you want to buy yourself some vodka or whiskey,' I fired back at her.

"She gaped at me, raised her finger to point and then looked at Rodney, who was staring up at her with his eyes full of fear. It slowed her down and all she did was shake her head.

" 'You two kids are punishment for me, that's all. I'm being punished for having you.'

" 'What should we say, Momma? We don't drink and get into fights at One-Eyed Bill's. I don't bring a man home to be in my bed,' I said, the tears streaming down my cheeks, 'look how we're being punished.'

" 'You're a regular smarty pants,' she said nodding her head slowly. 'Okay, don't feel sorry for me, a woman with kids deserted. I only hope nothing like this happens to you someday. Then you'll be sorry for what you say to me,' she whined. 'I do my best with what little I have.'

"She sat herself down and sobbed. Rodney, who started trembling and crying himself, went to her when she held open her arms and she clung to him, crying over him, trying to make me feel like I was the bad one. In the end I did say I was sorry and she cried about how she wished she could do more for her old, sick mother, but she was just overwhelmed and I should be understanding.

"I didn't say anything more. A little less than a week later, Granny went home from the hospital. We went to visit her and she did seem okay. Most of the visit, Momma complained about her own problems anyway, so Granny wouldn't have had a chance to talk about herself much even if it was in her nature to do so, which it wasn't.

"I checked on her as much as I could, took the bus to see her whenever I had the chance, and then, as I told you, Aaron moved in and our lives were turned even more topsy-turvy for a while.

"Before Daddy had left, Momma at least did a little something for Rodney and me. There were times she did the cooking and she went shopping for stuff we needed. Sometimes, when she drank, she got all maudlin and sobbed, clinging to Rodney and acting as if she was sorry for us. That was about the only time she gave him any real affection.

"I was always more or less on my own, but at least she cared something about him.

"However, after she started with Aaron, she acted more and more like a woman without any responsibilities. Everything that had to be done for us was an effort. She wanted to be free to party and sleep late every morning.

"I got so I didn't care. As I said, I didn't have

any social life of my own. I never went to a school party and rarely went to the movies. If I did, I'd have to take Rodney along with me because Momma was never there to watch him at night, especially on the weekend.

"Her conscience reared its weak head from time to time, but when it did, she moaned and groaned about how she had been cheated of her youth by a man who had made her pregnant with me. When Daddy was there, she'd try to make him feel guilty about it. He used to say, 'From the way you talk, Aretha, people might think I raped you.'

"And she would counter with, 'That's what it was. You didn't tie me down, but you tricked me, Kenny Fisher. You bedazzled me before I had enough sense to stop you.'

"He'd laugh at that. He'd look at me and laugh at her. Yesterday, Misty, you were talking about how your parents complained about each other to you. That's what mine did, too, only I was too young to understand most of it. Daddy would turn to me as he laughed and talk about Momma and then she would turn to me and do the same and I'd look from one to the other, not knowing whether I should smile, laugh or burst into tears. Yeah, I got so I wanted to put my hands over my ears like you, too.

"It got so I didn't have to, though. I'd stop hearing them even though they were shouting at me. I didn't see them either. I know because suddenly, I'd blink and discover they were both gone. Daddy had left the house and Momma was in the bedroom mumbling to the mirror.

"I didn't have my magic carpet then, but I guess I still left."

I reached for my glass of water and took a sip. How different all their faces were now, I thought. Jade didn't look as arrogant to me anymore. Misty had lost that cute smile and Cat, who looked everywhere but at me most of the time, stared with eyes that were full of sympathy and understanding.

"One day Aaron and Momma started talking about a vacation they wanted to take. They were planning on driving north to San Francisco where Aaron supposedly had some acquaintances who owed him a good time. The plan was to leave us with Granny. I didn't mind that. I was actually looking forward to it.

"But a few days later, Rodney was burning up with fever when I went to wake him in the morning. He was so hot, my fingers actually jumped back from his cheeks. I couldn't get him to really wake up. He groaned and his eyes were so glassy, I couldn't imagine him seeing anything.

"I shouted for Momma who immediately started complaining about being woken until I got her into the bedroom and she touched him herself. She looked real scared and that made me more afraid.

" 'We better get him over to the hospital emergency room,' " she said and went back to wake

Aaron. Both of them looked like they were the ones with fevers. Aaron practically had to have his eyelids pinned open. We wrapped Rodney in his blanket and Momma carried him out to Aaron's car.

"I'd been to the emergency room a few times before in my life besides that time with Rodney when he needed stitches. It was always crowded with people, each one looking sicker than the next. Everyone in the waiting lounge is coughing or sneezing, moaning and looking like they're moments away from dying, so even though Rodney was so bad, we couldn't get him any immediate attention. We sat there for nearly two hours. Aaron fell asleep in his chair and Momma got into one of her mean moods and bitched so much, she made the nurses furious at her.

"I thought Rodney would be the one to suffer for that. They wouldn't rush to help us now. I tried to tell her that. Granny always says you can get more with honey than you can with vinegar, but Momma was just so angry her life had been disrupted, she wanted to take it out on anyone she could.

"Finally, they called us in and the doctor began to examine Rodney. They had to run tests and we were there for nearly five more hours before the doctor came out to see Momma to tell her Rodney had an infection in his spinal cord.

" 'I think we're going to get to it in time with antibiotics to prevent a really serious situation, but he's a sick little boy for now,' he said.

" 'Well, why the hell you make us wait out here so long? I knew that boy was sick. I just knew it. Mommas know these things,' she lectured.

" 'There are many sick people here, Mrs. Fisher,' the doctor said calmly. 'We do the best we can.'

"Of course that wasn't good enough for her. She just repeated herself. Finally, he left us to get Rodney into treatment. He said Rodney would be there most of the week, which set her off on another stream of complaints. Now her vacation was ruined.

"I should tell you that once in a while, Momma would be in a good mood. After she had begun with Aaron, she seemed to have more smiles and she'd sing around the house the way she used to when I was a little girl. I got so I concluded Aaron was a good thing for her and therefore, for me and Rodney.

"But Rodney's getting sick just as she was about to have what she called her first 'real vacation,' turned the clock back and she was meaner and nastier than ever. She had already told One-Eyed Bill's she was taking off so she was home more and all she did was drink and complain.

"I was at the hospital visiting Rodney more than she was because two of the days that week, she had drunk herself into a coma.

"Rodney's illness seemed to seal up a decision working in the back of her head, that and the eviction notice we got."

"She wasn't paying her rent?" Jade asked. "But

she was working, wasn't she?"

"Yeah, well I didn't know much about our bills. I remembered the phone being shut off twice and once we had no electric because she hadn't paid the bills, but she eventually got around to it and things were all right again.

"About three days after Rodney came home from the hospital, someone knocked on our door and I opened it to find a man in a suit asking for my mother. I told him she was at work and he smirked and said, 'If she's working, why doesn't she pay the rent?'

"I didn't have any answer for him. He handed me an envelope and said I should be sure she gets it. After he left, I opened it and read the warning that we were to be evicted in thirty days unless all the back rent was paid. In my heart I knew it would never be, but I had no idea what the solution cooking in Momma's brain was.

"When she came home, I gave her the notice. She read it and then crumbled it up and threw it in the garbage.

" 'What are we going to do about it, Momma?' I asked her.

" 'Nothing. Don't worry about it,' she said. She wouldn't say anything more about it.

"At the end of the week, she announced that she and Aaron had rescheduled their 'real vacation,' and she had made arrangements again with Granny.

" 'But how are we going to go to school?' I asked her. 'Granny lives too far away from where

Rodney and I go to school.'

" 'You can miss some school so I can get a holiday,' she snapped back at me.

" 'The school's not going to like that,' I warned her, but she was about as worried about that as she was about our eviction notice.

"I was too tired to care anymore about school anyway. I was doing poorly in most of my subjects, failing math. The counselor had been calling me in at least twice a month, but even she seemed to give up on me. There are a lot of kids with problems in my school. After a while no one even noticed me. I bet they didn't even realize I was gone.

"Momma made me pack up most of Rodney's things and my own and then she and Aaron drove us to Granny's apartment. It's a smaller apartment than the one we were in, but it was on the ground floor and Granny had a small patch of ground behind it, almost a real backyard. Rodney and I would have to continue to share a bedroom, which was really Granny's sewing room that had a pull-out bed. Aaron had squeezed Rodney's cot-bed into his car trunk, so we at least had that.

"Momma went into this big act before she left, warning Rodney and me to behave while she was away. 'You're here to help Granny,' she said, and made that look like the main reason she had brought us.

" 'We'll call you in a day or so, Momma,' she told Granny and they left. She gave Rodney a quick peck on the cheek, but she just looked at me as if I was miles and miles away. There was something in her eyes that caused a flutter of panic in me. My heart skipped and my stomach felt as if it had filled with hot tears.

"Sometimes, I could look at Momma when she was unaware and I could catch a glimpse of who and what she had been when I was much younger. It was almost as if the face she wore now was really a mask and under it was the face of the Momma I had known and once loved like a Momma should be loved. Her eyes would twinkle and her lips would soften into a small smile. It warmed my heart and made me feel safe, if only for a little while.

"I saw that face glimmer for a moment as she stood in the doorway looking back at me. I wanted to run up to her and embrace her and get a real hug of love from her, but it passed and the mask came back strong.

" 'You take care of everyone,' she ordered.

" 'I always do,' I muttered, which she didn't like. She turned to Aaron and they left quickly.

"Momma didn't call the next day and most of the day after that. Then, just after we had eaten our dinner, the phone rang and it was finally her calling.

"I saw that Granny was doing more listening than speaking and keeping her eyes on me and Rodney as she did so.

" 'No,' she said. 'That so? You didn't tell me about that, Aretha. Of course I will,' she added.

113

"I was waiting nearby, wondering if Momma would ask to speak to me or to Rodney, but she didn't. Granny finally said good-bye and hung up.

" 'What's wrong now, Granny?' I asked.

" 'Your momma says you were all evicted from the apartment. You know about that?'

" 'Yeah, I do. I was home when the man brought the notice,' I said, 'and she told me not to worry about it.'

" 'Well, you lost your home,' Granny said.

"Rodney didn't understand it, but he knew it was bad so he just started to cry and I went to him and held him.

" 'What is she going to do about it, Granny?' I asked.

" 'She said she and Aaron are going to try to set up a home for you all in San Francisco. Aaron's been promised new work with some friends of his and she's looking for work too. Once they settle into a new place, they'll send for you,' Granny added.

"She might have even believed it when she told me then, but after a few days of not hearing from Momma, I could see the trust evaporating. Momma called once more the following week and gave basically the same story. When she didn't call at all the next week, Granny decided we should enroll in the closest schools and she saw that we did.

"Another week went by and another. Momma called once in a while with a different story.

Then she called to say she and Aaron were thinking of trying their luck on the East Coast. Aaron had an uncle who owned a convenience store in Wilmington, Delaware and needed help. He supposedly said there was a lot of work Momma could get, too.

"Granny didn't believe her, but she looked at Rodney and me and I guess she thought what was happening was for the best. After she hung up that time, she and I talked about it and she said, 'Well, I guess I'll have to stay in this world a little longer than I had expected.'

" 'I guess you better, Granny,' I told her.

"So I became what Misty called yesterday a OWP, orphan with parents. Good riddance to them both, I say."

I paused, looked at the ceiling and then at Doctor Marlowe. I could see she was waiting for me to tell them, so I got up my courage and I did.

"My troubles," I admitted, "were just starting."

6

"As I said before, Granny wanted us to enroll in new schools and we did. I couldn't help being upset with all the changes in our lives. Rodney was bothered even more than I was, but rather than just clam up the way Daddy often did, he began to misbehave, deliberately breaking things in class, getting into fights and talking back to his new teachers. Twice the first month Granny had to go to school because of things he had done. He had grown up in a house with a mother who threw things when she was angry and didn't hesitate to use bad language in front of him, mostly because she had been drinking and didn't even realize what she was saying, so I guess he didn't have what you would call a good role model.

"Nevertheless, I tried being angry at him and bawling him out for the things he did, but when he turned his lost, lonely eyes on me, I stopped yelling and just hugged him. Finally, I got to him a little by telling him I was worried more about

116

Granny's health than I was about him or me.

" 'Remember, she had one heart attack. She could have another and then where will we be? We'll be in some institution, that's where.' I told him.

"He seemed to understand that and calmed down enough so he didn't get into trouble, but his schoolwork didn't improve any.

"Neither did mine. The bad habits followed me, I guess. I didn't see how I could ever do anything for myself with studies, and when counselors asked me if I had any idea what I wanted to be or do, I just shook my head and stared out the window. The future was as cloudy as could be. It amazed me how anyone could look years and years beyond today and see what he or she would be doing. I just worried about tomorrow.

"I made some new friends quickly. Everyone's curious about a new student and asks questions and lots of kids were in situations like mine. I knew I was far from the only one who was living with her granny or granny and grandpa. One of the girls, Tina Carter, had a cousin in my previous school who had been a friend of mine so Tina and I became friendly and she told me stuff about many of the other kids, especially the boys to avoid because of their criminal records or gangs they were in.

"One boy she warned me about, Steve Gilmore, was interesting and attractive to me nevertheless. Tina said he was weird. He liked to be alone. He didn't have any real friends at the school and nobody knew much about him or saw him on weekends at the usual hangouts. The only one he seemed to spend any time with at school was a white boy, Matthew Langer, who had such severe learning disabilities he had been held back two grades. The fact that he would rather spend his time talking to Matthew than anybody else made him more interesting to me. It was sort of understood that Steve protected him too.

"Steve wasn't all that big and strong looking. He was just under six feet and only about one hundred and seventy pounds, but he had a wildness in his eyes that made other boys give him space. I guess it was because of the way he fixed his gaze on someone. People said they felt like he was burning into them. Someone had nicknamed him 'Laser Eyes' and the name stuck, but no one called him that to his face.

"There were all sorts of stories about him that were practically mythical."

"Like what?" Jade asked.

"He supposedly had killed someone in a fight when he was only nine years old, stole a car and got into an accident that resulted in the death of a young woman, stuff like that.

"However, from what I could tell, Steve wasn't in trouble much in school. He was an okay student, quiet and not disrespectful when his teachers approached him. I had one class with him, social studies. I would glance his way from time to time. He sat just behind me about two rows over, but he never seemed to look at me or take the slightest interest in me.

"I had begun to take better care of myself, fix my hair, wear some lipstick, polish my nails. Granny managed to get me some nicer clothes too. She did seamstress work for a department store sometimes and the manager got us some deep discounts.

"Granny told me I was pretty. I guessed she was saying that because she was my granny, but Tina told me she and her girlfriends had decided I was one of the prettiest girls in the school now. If that was so, I wondered why Steve Gilmore never gave me a first look, not to mention a second. I wasn't much interested in the other boys who had.

"What I would do occasionally in class was lean back on a slant so I could gaze at Steve without it looking too obvious. I guess another thing that attracted me to him was a look I saw occasionally in his eyes that suggested he was hurting in places I was hurting. He seemed to drift away, too.

"I know from the way you're all looking at me that it's hard to understand what I mean. Some-times, I'd catch a glimpse of myself in a mirror and I'd do a double-take because there was this deep, dark shadow in my eyes that made them look like tiny tunnels running back to my most painful childhood memories. I'd be surprised at how much time went by with me looking down those tunnels. I guess we called them 'flashbacks,' right, Doctor Marlowe?"

She nodded.

"It would start with me thinking of myself as being five or six and wondering who was this looking at me in the mirror? Then I would just fall back through time. The whole experience leaves you with this heavy sadness, like a water-soaked blanket being tossed on your shoulders."

They all stared, no one speaking.

"I don't do a good job of explaining it," I added.

"Yes, you do," Jade said quickly.

I smiled at her and nodded.

"Anyway, when I looked at Steve one time like this, he turned slowly and looked at me for a moment. It was like we had said hello in a very private way and recognized we were from the same planet, Planet Pain."

Misty looked mesmerized, but her lips stretched slowly into a tiny smile.

"I live there too," she whispered.

I nodded at her, encouraged by how many similar notes we all heard.

"Something happened at that special moment I looked at Steve," I continued. "It was like he had opened his eyes or become conscious and finally noticed me. As it turned out, he wasn't weird so much as he was just very shy. It took another two days before he would utter a word in my direction. I was walking home after school, on my way to stop at Rodney's school and pick him up, when Steve came up behind me and

120

passed me, but paused for a split second to say, 'Hi' He kept walking, faster in fact, before I could respond. In seconds, he was gone around the corner, but it was enough to give my heart a tiny nudge and make me think about him all that night.

"The next day I became bold and when I saw him in the hallway just before social studies, I stepped up beside him and asked him if he had done the homework. We were supposed to describe four causes for World War One.

"He gave me those 'laser eyes' for a second as if he distrusted my intentions. Those remarkable eyes practically drank me in and swallowed me down before he relaxed.

" 'I only came up with three,' he replied.

" 'I only got down three causes, too,' I said.

"I told him mine and he told me his and between us we came up with five to use. When I got to my desk, I quickly scribbled it all down, looking over at him every few seconds to see him doing the same. He gave me a smile and I felt as if he had kissed me."

"Just a smile did that to you?" Cat asked. She had been so quiet and unmoving, I forgot about her for a while. As usual, she glanced from right to left in a small panic because her words had come out so fast.

"He had a really nice smile. His whole face would change, warm up and look more than just friendly. His eyes were laughing, full of sparkling light. He was . . ."

"Sexy?" Misty offered.

"No, not just that. It was full of understanding. That's it. I felt we spoke and thought alike. Granny has this expression 'birds of a feather.' She often looks at people in the street and says, 'Them two are birds of a feather.' People make fun of older people who have all these funny sayings and such, but some of them were dipped in a well of wisdom and make lots of sense. At least to me," I added.

"So?" Jade asked impatiently. "What happened after this great smile?"

"You can make fun all you want," I said, "but sometimes people say more with one look than they do with a thousand words."

"I'm not making fun. I just want to know what happened next," she insisted. She blew air through her lips and shook her head at me.

I glanced at Doctor Marlowe, who just wore that infuriating look of patience, waiting for one of us to throw a tantrum.

"After class Steve and I finally got into a conversation," I said, my voice taut and strained until I began remembering. "It continued into lunch and I sat with him and Matthew, who looked upset about it the whole time, practically eating nothing."

"He was jealous of the time you were taking with his only friend, huh?" Misty asked.

"I guess. I tried to be nice to him, but he looked angry no matter what. It took another few days of conversation before I found out that

Steve's mother had been killed in a car accident about five years ago and he lived with his father and had no brothers or sisters, but I could tell from the way he spoke about his father that things were bad.

"Later, I would learn that it was his father who was driving the car and he was drunk. He was cited for DWI and actually charged with vehicular manslaughter, but he got probation, probably because of Steve losing his mother.

"We began to talk every chance we got at school. Sometimes, we ate lunch outside and really felt we had privacy because the other kids weren't staring at us and whispering. Eventually, I felt comfortable enough to tell him about my life, what had happened with my daddy and momma and such. He was less open about his life. If I asked him a question, he would look away, maybe eat some of his food, and then finally give me a short answer. I could tell pretty fast what he would talk about and what he wouldn't."

"What about Matthew all this time?" Cat asked.

"He followed us around sometimes and after a while, he was nicer to me.

"And then Steve asked me on a date. I guess it wasn't a date exactly, but it was the first time I had a boy ask to come by and get me to go someplace with him."

"He had his own car?" Jade asked skeptically.

"No. We were taking the Big Blue Bus," I said.

"The poor people's limousine," I added dryly. She pursed those pretty lips and gazed at the ceiling.

"Where did you go?" Misty asked.

"To the Santa Monica pier. I asked Granny if I could go and then Rodney got all excited about it and I had to take him, too, but that was another thing I liked about Steve. He didn't mind Rodney being along. In fact, he felt better because he was coming along, I think. I think he was real nervous about being alone with me and jumped at the chance to be like a big brother more than a boyfriend.

"Of course, Rodney ate it up. I laughed to myself at the way he immediately looked up to Steve, hanging on his every word as if Steve was one of his television heroes or something. Then I thought to myself, Rodney never had a real father long enough to appreciate him and of course, he had no older brother, and Aaron was nothing to him. I was okay as his sister, but it wasn't the same thing for a little boy. No wonder he was so excited about the attention Steve gave him.

"They got this fun park on the pier. You all probably know about it."

They all nodded.

"Taking Rodney on the rides was fun for both of us. Steve insisted on paying for everything no matter how much I protested. He told me there was some money put aside in a trust for him from his mother's life insurance so he would have something with which to start when he got out of high school, and for now his father gave him a generous allowance because he was responsible for buying things they needed, food and such.

"We talked about what we'd do after we graduated. I still had no idea, but he thought he might enlist in the army. Because of his trust he was secure about his future, knowing he had something he could depend upon.

" 'My father can't get his hands on it, either,' he pointed out. 'My mother was smart enough to know my father wasn't going to provide all that well for us and she believed she'd be working her whole life too, just to make ends meet,' he said. 'She made sure I'd be all right.'

"His eyes always filled with tears when he talked about his momma, but he knew it was happening and snapped those lids like two rubber bands and brought that famous hard, cold look back into them.

"At the pier, he really seemed to be enjoying Rodney, laughing at the way Rodney's face filled with pure ecstasy at the prospect of going from one ride to the other, getting a hot dog and a cotton candy, playing machines in the arcade, trying to win cheap prizes that you'd be better off just going out and buying.

"I guess after a while I was jealous."

"Jealous?" Misty asked, jumping on what I had said. "Why should you be jealous of hot dogs, cotton candy and pinball machines?"

"It wasn't that. Steve seemed more excited about having fun with Rodney than being with me." I looked at Doctor Marlowe. She and I had discussed this and worked it out, I thought.

"Maybe he was just socially immature," Jade interjected. "You said he was shy."

"It wasn't that, either," I replied quickly. "He never got to be a little boy like Rodney was and have fun like this. He was having a, what did you call it again?" I asked Doctor Marlowe. "Vicarry . . . vi . . ."

"A vicarious experience," Doctor Marlowe said.

"Yeah, that. He was doing stuff through Rodney, being the little boy he wished he was."

"It amazes me how everyone's a psychoanalyst nowadays," Jade said smugly.

"Oh, and I suppose you don't do that?" Misty attacked. "You don't analyze everything?"

"He was probably just shy," Jade insisted. "Oh, what difference does it make what he was?"

"No difference to you, but a lot to her," Misty offered. Jade glanced at me and realized that might be so. Her expression changed.

"He ignored you the whole time?" she asked in a softer voice. "Some first date that turned out to be, I suppose. Boys can be so aggravating."

"I didn't say he ignored me. He was into doing things with Rodney more, that's all. I admit I was jealous and wished he paid more attention to me, but I saw how much fun Rodney was having and he hadn't had much fun in his life till then, so I

126

wasn't about to complain.

"Afterward, Rodney sat on the beach and played in the sand while Steve and I took off our shoes and let the water run over our feet.

" 'Thanks for what you done for my brother today,' I told him.

"He nodded and looked out over the ocean and said he'd never been to the pier before. I was surprised to hear that.

" 'Me and my father never really went anywhere together, anywhere that was fun for me, that is. I've been to his friends' houses with him and such, but he never took me anywhere that was fun for me.'

"He said he could barely remember the places he went with his momma.

"Then he looked back at Rodney and said, 'I know what it's like for him growing up with a drunk for a parent.'

" 'Your daddy still drinks a lot?' I asked. I knew how hard it was to answer that question when someone put it to you, but I thought how could his father still drink after what had happened. Steve laughed.

" 'Still drinks a lot? You remember when you told me how as a little girl you thought the smell of whiskey on your momma was just her perfume?'

" 'Yes,' I said.

" 'Well, I grew up thinking whiskey came out of the kitchen faucet. I still wonder if it does,' he said. 'What difference does it make?' he added

127

quickly. 'He'll die soon and put himself out of his misery.'

" 'You hate him?' I asked.

Of course, when he had told me about his mother and the accident, I just imagined he would blame his father forever.

But when he looked at me, those eyes were a mixture of hard, cold anger and some sorrow, too.

" 'I don't care about him enough to hate him,' he said. 'I don't even think about him much if I can help it.'

" 'But you live in the same house with him,' I said. 'You see each other every day, don't you?'

" 'We're more like two people renting some rooms together. I'm usually out of there before he gets up to go to work and I have my supper before he gets home most of the time.'

" 'You cook for yourself?'

" 'Yeah. The cook quit,' he said. He was quiet for a moment and then he added, 'He eats my food, too, when he wants to eat at home.'

" 'I'm impressed,' I said.

"He laughed. He had a nice laugh when he allowed it. It was like it was shut up in his heart and he opened the door just a little and let happiness breathe. Sadness can be more like a disease. It makes you sick anyway."

Without doubt the three of them understood that, I thought.

"Anyway, he turned to me and said, 'Why don't you come over for dinner tomorrow night?

I make a great frozen pot pie.'

" 'Frozen? Some cook. I'm a cook, too,' I said. 'Not as good as Granny, but a lot better than my momma. I'll prepare the salad and Granny will let me bake an apple pie to bring.'

"His eyes looked like Rodney's when Rodney set them on the fun park.

" 'Really? You'll make an apple pie and come?'

" 'I don't say I'm gonna do something if I don't mean to do it,' I told him with my eyes fixed as hard and firm as his could be.

" 'Okay,' he said, smiling, 'Okay. It's a date,' he said.

"I laughed, but I was more than just happy about it. I was excited. Funny, how little things like that can give you so much hope," I muttered and reached for my water.

No one spoke. They all watched me drink.

"Granny got a saying for hope," I told them. "She says hope is what you cast out like a fish line and hook, hoping to pull in some happiness, but if you cast it too far or too often, the line snaps and you watch it all float away."

"What's all that supposed to mean?" Misty asked, scrunching up her nose.

"It means if you spend all your time dreaming and hoping, you'll be disappointed. You've got to work hard at being happy and not expect it'll just come floating along and bite your hook," I said.

Doctor Marlowe smiled.

"Maybe we should be sitting around with her

grandmother," Jade offered dryly.

"It hasn't hurt Star," Doctor Marlowe said.

Jade pulled in the corner of her mouth. She looked like her eyes were tearing up.

Suddenly, I realized something about her. She has nobody, I thought. That's it. That's what makes her so mean and nasty sometimes.

Maybe she's not so rich after all.

7

"At first, Granny wasn't going to let me go to Steve's house for dinner.

" 'What do you mean you and this boy are going to make dinner for yourselves and you want to make a pie? Where's his momma? Why doesn't she cook?' she wanted to know.

"I explained what had happened to Steve's mother without telling her about his father and his drinking. I knew that would spook her, but she started to ask more and more questions about his father until I had to admit that I didn't know very much about him.

" 'You are going over to that man's house to eat his supper and you don't know anything about him? What if he doesn't want you there? I don't like this,' she said shaking her head.

" 'Granny, if there's any problem, I swear I'll just leave and come right back,' I promised.

" 'Why don't you bring this boy around here first?' she suggested. 'I'll cook him a meal.'

" 'He's too shy, Granny. He won't come.'

" 'He's too shy to come here, but not too shy to invite you there?' she asked, her eyes narrowing with worry and suspicion.

" 'He's living on his own, Granny. His daddy's not there much.'

" 'I don't like the sound of that, Star,' she said shaking her head.

" 'I won't get into trouble, Granny,' I told her. 'You don't think I'm a good girl? You don't think you can trust me?'

" ' 'Course I do,' she said, 'but sometimes things happen anyway.'

" 'I like him, Granny. He's a nice boy. He was good to Rodney and you know from what you heard Rodney say that Rodney likes him, too.'

" 'You want to take Rodney with you?' she asked. I couldn't tell if that would make her happier or more reluctant.

" 'No, Granny. I want to have some time to myself. Thanks to Momma, I never really did,' I said. 'I'm nearly sixteen,' I told her, 'and I haven't even been out on a real date.'

"I hated to sound like I was whining, but that was what I was doing. Granny gave it more thought and I guess she concluded I did deserve some freedom. We hadn't heard from Momma in a long time and there was little hope she would come back soon for me and Rodney. Together, Granny and I had a lot of responsibility now.

" 'Well, you call me if you have to leave and you be extra careful, Star. I don't have the strength to deal with some new big problem.'

" 'I know that better than you do, Granny. I keep telling you that you're doing too much, don't I? I tell you to leave the wash for me, but you do it all before I get home from school, and you hardly ever let me do any of the cooking, not to mention cleaning this place,' I reminded her.

"She looked at me and laughed.

" 'That's true enough,' she said. 'Okay. I'll help you make the pie,' she concluded and we set to doing it.

"Rodney was upset that he wasn't going along, but I promised him we would do something fun with him on the weekend and he settled for it.

"I don't think I was ever more excited about anything than I was about going to Steve Gilmore's house for dinner. I imagine it doesn't sound like much to you girls to go have frozen pot pies with a boy, but to me it was my Sweet Sixteen, a school prom, and a big fancy date all wrapped into one night."

"I would have thought it would be fun," Misty admitted with those big innocent eyes.

Jade looked away rather than comment and Cat looked like she agreed with Misty.

"So, after I brought Rodney home from school the next day, I packed up the salad and the pie and headed for the bus stop. I had to walk three blocks to Steve's neighborhood after I got off the bus and it wasn't the nicest section of the city. Some of the houses looked downright deserted. The streets were dirty and there were broken-down cars that looked like they had been left there for months.

"His house was small with just a patch of grass in the front. Some of the grass looked yellow and there were big dead spots. The front porch on the house leaned to one side like it had collapsed after an earthquake or the beams holding it up had just rotted: A front window had a crack in it and most of the siding was peeled and faded badly. The truth is when I first came upon it, I thought I might have the wrong address. I didn't think anyone lived in this one either.

"However, Steve must have been watching for me because the moment I turned into his short, chipped and broken cement sidewalk, he stepped out the front door.

" 'Welcome to my palace,' he said with a crooked smile, holding his arms out wide.

" 'How long have you lived here?' I asked trying not to sound too critical.

" 'Long as I can remember. It was my grandpa's house, my father's daddy. When he died, it was practically all he had to leave to him, I guess. Once it was nice. I know because I've seen some pictures.

" 'Well, come on inside. No sense in putting it off,' he added.

"You could tell two men lived there by themselves the moment you stepped through the door. The living room furniture needed a good dusting, the rugs were worn so thin in spots, you could see the wood floor beneath them. There were glasses and bottles on tables and the ash-trays were full of butts. On closer look I could see places where Steve's father had let a cigarette ash burn into the sofa or the easy chair. I knew his father must have done it because Steve didn't smoke and I also knew how careless Momma used to be when she drank and smoked.

"None of the windows had curtains, just shades, and the house itself had a musty, damp smell.

Jade grimaced as if she had stomach gas.

"The kitchen looked somewhat better, prob-ably because Steve had done some last minute cleaning in anticipation of my arrival. They had a round, badly chipped wooden table and chairs in it, a microwave as well as a stove and a refriger-ator that looked like it was threatening to drop dead. The motor made a small clang. The walls throughout the house needed a good whitewash, and in the kitchen, the linoleum floor was buck-ling in the corners and badly stained in many spots.

"There was little decoration on the walls, no flowers, no pictures, no knickknacks, no femi-nine touch anywhere. I had a glimpse of his fa-ther's room when he showed me the rest of the small house. There were clothes lying on the floor, over chairs and on the unmade bed. Steve's room was neat, but the furniture looked ready for the antique farm, if you know what I mean, dull finish, chipped and scratched, just like most of the pieces in the house. There was just an old, faded oval gray area rug beside his bed.

"Steve could see my reaction to his home. It's always hard for me to hide what I'm thinking. I've got a pair of eyes that might as well be magnifying glasses over my thoughts."

"You can say that again," Jade muttered.

I glared at her for a moment and then returned to telling them about Steve.

" 'When my mother was alive, this place looked decent at least,' he told me.

" 'I bet,' I said and he laughed at how I had said it. 'I mean you and your father aren't much at housekeeping.'

" 'He ain't much at anything,' Steve muttered. 'Hungry?' he asked.

" 'Sure,' I said and we went about preparing our dinner. He was excited about the pie. I told him my granny had made the crust. It was her specialty and no matter how much I tried, I couldn't get it as good. He liked hearing me talk about Granny, how she fidgeted over her home cooking, her stories about her own mother and father, and of course, her famous sayings.

"When I asked him about his grandparents, he could only remember his father's daddy. He had never seen his mother's parents; they had both died before he was five or six.

"I wondered why he didn't have any brothers or sisters and he said, 'Just luck.'

"I was going to laugh when I saw how serious he was about it.

" 'Can you imagine if there was another kid in

this house, especially younger, like Rodney? You know what things have been like for him,' he said and we sat and talked a little more about life with an alcoholic for a parent. That's when I realized even more that we really were birds of a feather," I said and paused.

"Why?" Jade asked. She didn't want to give me a moment's rest, it seemed. Why was she so damn anxious to hear all my story? I had come this morning thinking they all wouldn't be interested in my poor girl's life, and they seemed more interested in me than in Misty and maybe themselves.

"Because of the feelings he had about it, the kind of things he thought.

" 'I used to feel like smashing things,' he told me. 'My father was drunk so much, I was sure he didn't care about me. Counselors and such always told me I couldn't do anything about his problem. He was sick. They wanted me to think of him as suffering some diseases, you know.

" 'I'm not religious,' he said, 'but I couldn't help wondering why God let this happen to me and especially to my momma. You ever think that?'

" 'Lots of times,' I told him. 'Granny used to tell me it's all just a test and we should feel sorry for those who are hurting us.'

" 'You believe that?' he asked quickly. I didn't want to say I did. I knew he didn't.

" 'Sometimes,' I admitted, 'but not often.'

"He laughed and talked about all the times he

137

thought about running away.

" 'I almost did last year,' he said, 'but I talked to this counselor at school, Mr. VanVleet, and he said, "Just accept it, Steve. Accept it and move on with your own life. When your father's ready to help himself, he will, or if he won't, you can't make him."

" 'I thought that made sense so I tried doing what he suggested and I ignored my father as much as I could. If he wasn't home to eat, too bad. If he fell over and slept on the floor most of the night, tough, even if he threw up over himself. For a little while, it was like a truce or something in here. We didn't talk much and we didn't see each other much when he was sober.'

" 'Did it help any?' I asked.

" 'Some, I think. He drank less for a while and started to act like he cared about me, you know. He'd ask how's your schoolwork? What do you want to do with yourself after you finish school? Questions I guess other parents ask their kids all the time.

" 'And then . . .' He paused and looked like he wasn't going to go on.

" 'What?' I pushed.

" 'He got mixed up with a woman who drinks more than he does. I can't stand her. A lot of garbage comes out of her mouth and when he turns his back or leaves her alone with me, she . . .'

" 'She what?' I asked.

" 'Never mind,' he said. 'Luckily, most of the time he's at her place. That's probably where he's at tonight,' he told me.

"He was so full of rage, he made my anger look like a little drizzle. We were both quiet for a long moment, both trying to keep our blood calm.

" 'What does your father do for work now?' I asked him. He had told me his father once had a good job with the water department but got fired because he came in late too often and drunk once.

" 'He works at a garage. I think it's a chop shop, myself,' he added.

"I asked him what that was and he said a place where they bring stolen cars to tear off parts and sell them. Of course, that frightened me a little, but he shrugged and said, 'Like the man told me, ignore him.'

"In the fading, purplish light of the falling day, his glimmering eyes met with mine and we stared at each other for a long moment. Though I knew his heart had been shredded even worse than mine, I could sense his longing to put it together and fill it with some sort of love and he knew what I was thinking. Like I said," I added with a small smile, "two magnifying glasses on my thoughts.

" 'You're a really nice girl,' he said.

" 'Thank you,' I told him.

" 'I don't mean just nice,' he continued. 'I mean you're pretty in and out.'

"I smiled, not really knowing what he meant. He looked frustrated with his attempt to express himself.

" 'Granny's always telling me I'm pretty,' I said.

" 'She's right of course, but I mean more. There are lots of good-looking girls at our school, I guess, but they're just beautiful on the outside. Your beauty goes deep. Yours is where it really counts,' he said.

"I thanked him again. He felt awkward so we talked about dinner and set the table. Together with the salad and some fresh bread he had bought, our pot pies tasted pretty good. Afterward, we had the apple pie and he had some ice cream to put on it. We both had seconds.

" 'I bet you think I'm a pig,' I said. 'I don't usually eat like this.'

" 'I think when you feel happy, you have a bigger appetite,' he said. I agreed and I told him how I thought sadness was like a sickness. I couldn't believe how easy it was to talk with him now and how much I wanted to tell him. The more we talked, the closer I felt to him.

" 'When we got up to put the dishes in the sink, we stood really close to each other and we kissed. It was just a short kiss. I call it a test kiss. You throw your lips out there and see what happens."

"What happened?" Misty asked.

"We kissed again, longer, and then . . ."

"You forgot about the dishes," Jade said with a slow, know-it-all nod. Her eyes were bright and sharp and full of her own experiences.

"Exactly," I said.

Misty's smile widened into a small laugh. Cat

looked like she was turning white from holding her breath so long.

A wry smile twisted Jade's lips.

"Thought so," she said with great self-satisfaction.

"Yeah, but what you think happened, didn't happen."

"Ever?" she challenged.

"That night," I said and she sat back, still quite pleased with herself.

After a beat of silence, Misty asked, "Why didn't it?"

"His daddy came home," I said, "and things got very unpleasant very quickly."

Jade's eyebrows rose. Cathy bit down on her lower lip. Doctor Marlowe sipped some water and stared at me. I could almost hear her asking herself, "Would I go on?"

"Steve and I cleaned up the kitchen, neither of us saying very much. Every once in a while, we would look into each other's eyes and pause. My heart started a heavy, faster beat that grew louder and harder every time he and I grazed each other. It was like electricity was in the air.

"I know a lot of people, especially other girls my age, look at me and think I've been with a lot of boys, but I'd never had anything like a boy-friend before I met Steve. I had crushes on boys and some had crushes on me, but nothing had ever come of it.

"I read enough romance stories and stuff and had been around Momma enough to know about sex and such, but when it's you, really you, it's different."

"That's for sure," Misty said. Cat looked at her for a moment and then turned back quickly to me, anticipating.

"We just held hands first. It was like both our palms had magnets in them or something. My hand practically floated into his and next thing I knew, we were walking toward his room, neither of us saying a word.

"When we got there, he let go and flopped on his bed, on his back, looking up at the ceiling with his hands behind his head.

" 'I guess you know what it's like for me laying around in my room and hearing my father bang into things when he comes home from a night out there,' he said. 'I hear him cursing and ranting. Sometimes, I can hear him crying through the wall. That's how he comes down from a drunk.'

" 'He feels bad about what happened with your mother,' I said.

"Steve opened his eyes wider and looked at me.

" 'Yeah, I suppose,' he said. 'Maybe that's why he drinks more and more now, to forget. Only, I don't think it helps you forget. I think it makes it come back, only like some . . . some nightmare.'

" 'I suppose you're right,' I said.

"I sat beside him and he brought his hands around and took my right hand into his and just held it, studying my fingers as if they was something special. Then he looked up at me again, his eyes practically speaking to me, drawing me toward him. I didn't even realize I had leaned so far over we were close enough to kiss again until we did.

"Suddenly I was beside him on the bed and he was hovering over me, his face so serious it made my heart skip beats until he brought his lips to mine again and then, when he touched me and unbuttoned my blouse, my heart felt more like a wild, frantic animal in my chest, thundering hard against my ribs. I was scared but excited.

"It didn't take long to get half undressed. The whole time I kept thinking Granny might be mad. I told her I was a good girl and she shouldn't worry and now look what I'm doing. But some other voice inside me said I was still a good girl. This wasn't wrong. I wanted to be loved. I needed to be loved.

"And so did Steve. We were giving something precious to each other, something we had been denied too long, and I don't just mean sex," I added quickly, my eyes throwing warning darts at Jade, but she didn't look like she was about to ridicule me anyway. She looked sad and excited and full of sympathy, all at once.

"I loved his lips all over me. I would have given myself to him right then and there. I know it was foolish to be like that and not to think of protection. I was aware of all that, but now I understood firsthand why some girls forget or lose control. I remember I was the impatient one, pushing myself at him, helping him with my skirt zipper, struggling to get comfortable.

"He pulled back the blanket and I got under as he finished taking off his clothes. He was kissing me and caressing me and I was thinking I'm a woman now. I don't care what happens; I don't care.

"I felt him about to be in me when suddenly, we heard the door open, loud laughter and a chair or something get knocked over. Steve froze and then his face filled with fear. He pulled back.

" 'You better get dressed,' he said. 'That's him for sure.'

"I hurriedly did so. We heard a female voice, too.

" 'She's with him,' Steve said. 'It'll be worse,' he predicted.

"Now my heart was really pounding, but in a different way. It was more like a thump, a deep drum vibrating my bones. I had a cold chill up and down my spine. I wasn't quite finished dressing when the door crashed open and Steve's father stood there, wobbling and looking in at us.

"He was a big man, four or five inches taller than Steve and probably forty pounds heavier, with large facial features and a balding head. His eyes were a familiar bloodshot red and I thought to myself, all drunks look alike. He had that same slobbering lip, that same dazed, unsteady stance, that same stream of madness running through his brain like a polluted stream.

" 'Well now, lookie here,' he declared. 'The

boy got himself some action.'

" 'Shut up,' Steve told him.

"His father laughed and then a small, buxom woman came up beside him looking drunker than he did, her hair down, her pearl white blouse open so that her bosom was visible almost to the nipples. She had dark freckles over her caramel cheeks. She was attractive enough that I was surprised she was with Steve's father. Steve had apparently gotten his good looks mainly from his mother.

"His girlfriend laughed.

" 'Well, let him be,' she said. 'He needs all the experience he can get.'

" 'That's for sure. It's about time he had a girl-friend. I was beginning to think he wasn't all right,' his father declared and swayed.

" 'Shut your foul mouth!' Steve shouted at him.

"His father seemed to swell, his shoulders rising and his neck thickening.

" 'Who are you talking to, boy?'

" 'C'mon, let 'em be,' his girlfriend said and tried to pull him away, but Steve's father hovered there, so wide he almost filled the doorway. She tugged to no avail and walked away.

"Steve turned his back on his father.

" 'Don't you have a smart mouth,' his father warned pointing a finger that looked as wide as my hand.

" 'Come on,' Steve told me. 'Let's go.'

"I was very frightened, but I walked toward the

door with him. His father didn't move. He smiled instead and his eyes bounced from my terrified face down to my breasts, lingered for a moment and then went lower and lower to my feet before they traveled back upward, making me feel as if he could look right through my clothes.

" 'She's a nice one,' he said. 'What's she doing with you?'

"He laughed at his own stupid remark. Steve stepped between him and me and nudged him just enough to get him to step back so I could pass. I didn't see it, but his father slapped Steve on the back of his head. I heard it, but Steve didn't stop. He pushed me forward faster as his father began to rant.

" 'Who are you pushing, boy? You show me respect. I'm your father, hear? Who are you pushing?'

"We paused for a moment in the kitchen. His father's girlfriend was pouring herself some gin. She looked up at us.

" 'You're welcome to a nip,' she said, 'but not much more. I'm not saying you're too young. I just don't want to give it away.' She laughed.

" 'Keep it and drown in it,' Steve told her.

" 'What did you say to Debbie?' his father cried.

"Steve urged me on and we left the house quickly, Steve's father raging behind us, screaming, 'What did you say, boy? What did you say to Debbie?'

"We could hear her laughing. I was glad to shut the door on it all. We hurried down the sidewalk and into the street.

" 'I'll walk you to the bus stop and wait with you,' Steve said. 'Sorry about all that, but now you know what I live with.'

"I felt terrible for him, but I was also happy to be out of there and on my way home to Granny.

"At the bus stop, he sat with his head down, apologizing and swearing he was going to do something about it all.

" 'Don't get yourself into any trouble with him,' I advised. 'Soon enough you'll be on your own and you'll have your trust money and you can leave.'

" 'Not soon enough,' he said.

"Because the wait was long for the bus, we had time to calm down. I told him my granny had wanted him to come to our house for dinner.

" 'She really wants to meet you,' I said. 'Rodney's still talking about you all the time.'

"He laughed and promised he would come as soon as I asked Granny what night. I expected it would be on the weekend.

" 'Maybe the two of us can take Rodney someplace like the zoo or something and then come back for dinner,' I suggested.

"He said fine. The bus came. We kissed goodnight and I got on. He stood there on the sidewalk looking up at me until the bus started away, and then he turned and reluctantly walked back toward his house and what awaited him.

"Granny was right, I thought. I guess I could feel sorrier for someone else than I did for myself. I certainly felt that way for him that night."

I looked at the three others, their eyes unmoving, all looking like they were holding their breath under water.

"But I had no idea even then how bad it was all going to get for both of us."

8

"I waited for Steve at his locker the next morning until the last bell rang for homeroom. He never showed up for school all that day. Lunchtime, I called his house because I was worried about him, but the operator came on to say the phone had been disconnected.

" 'Why?' I screamed into the receiver.

"She cut me off and I fumed, frustrated. After school, I hurried Rodney home and shouted to Granny I had to go someplace and I would be back later. She called after me, but I practically ran out of the house. It started raining lightly, and I missed one bus connection and had to run in the drizzle nearly eight blocks to make another. It was almost five o'clock by the time I reached Steve's street. My hair was soaked and so were my clothes and sneakers.

"Nothing looked any different about the house from the way it had looked the day before, except now it was darker because of the overcast sky and no lights on inside. I knocked on the door and waited and then knocked again, louder. Finally, it opened and there stood Steve with a big bruise on his swollen right cheek. His eyes went from surprise to happiness to anger.

" 'What are you doing here?' he asked gruffly and turned away so I couldn't get a good view of his bruise.

" 'I was worried when you didn't show up at school. I tried to call you lunchtime, but the operator said your phone was disconnected.'

" 'It is. He didn't pay the bill again,' Steve said.

" 'My momma was always forgetting to do that too,' I said.

The rain started to get harder once more and the wind blew it in under the porch roof.

" 'Can I come inside?' I asked.

"He stepped back.

" 'Why are you keeping it so dark in here?' I asked immediately.

" 'I was in my room. I didn't even notice,' he said. He kept looking down at the floor.

" 'What happened, Steve? He hit you when you returned to the house yesterday, didn't he?' I asked him.

" 'I don't want to talk about it,' he said. 'You shouldn't have come.'

" 'Is he here?' I asked, thinking that was why he had said that.

" 'No, he's with Debbie. It's her birthday,' he told me. 'Just another excuse to get plastered.'

" 'I'm sorry, Steve,' I said. He turned to me.

150

" 'What are you sorry for?' he asked.

" 'Maybe I caused the trouble by coming here yesterday,' I said.

" 'Trouble was here long before you came,' he said. He finally smiled. 'I'd risk a lot more to have you here,' he added. 'Look at you,' he said finally taking a good look at me. 'You got drenched.'

" 'I know." I was beginning to feel chilled as the dampness soaked through my clothes and to my skin.

" 'Come on,' he said, 'I'll get you some clean towels. You can use my mother's old hair dryer. It still works,' he added and I followed him to his room.

"He brought me some towels and watched me dry my hair and then I started to take off my clothes. I thought I might throw them into his clothes dryer for twenty minutes. He just stood there looking at me and I kept undressing until I was completely naked."

I heard Misty suck some air through her lips. Cat was looking down as if she couldn't look at me when I told them these things. Only Jade looked pleased, that small, pretty smile on her lips again.

"Yes," I said to her. "It happened." I paused and she looked disappointed, afraid I wasn't going to tell her how and why.

"His face just seemed to soften. It was like all the hardness and pain evaporated before my eyes and he looked almost like a little boy.

"My skin was still damp from the wet clothes, but I didn't dry myself. The excitement flowed through me and warmed my heart.

" 'You're so beautiful,' he said and he came to me and we kissed. He scooped me up and gently placed me on his bed as he stepped back and undressed. Once again, we were both under his blanket, embracing, kissing.

"He stopped and said, 'Last night, after it was all over, I fell asleep dreaming about you, imagining us right here. I hoped and even prayed it might happen, and when I opened that door before and saw you standing there, you looked like a dream come true.'

" 'Even with my hair soaked? Didn't I look more like a drowned rat?' I asked him.

" 'Hardly,' he said. 'Usually, I wouldn't have any faith in dreams and prayers and hopes, but you made me believe when you came here yesterday,' he said, as if it had been an earth-shattering decision for me to do so. 'I guess I expected you'd be here, somehow, someway again.'

"To prove it he reached under the pillow and produced a condom. Of course, I had seen them and of course, I knew what it was for, but it frightened me for a moment and he saw that in my face.

" 'We don't have to go further if you don't want to,' he said."

"What did you say?" Misty blurted, impatient with the small pause. I couldn't help it. My heart was pounding, just telling them.

"I didn't say anything," I told her. "I just kissed him and that was enough of an answer. It wasn't as painful for me as it was for you and that wasn't because I wasn't a virgin or anything," I added quickly. "It's not the same for everyone.

"Afterward, we fell asleep in each other's arms. We slept like that for nearly an hour and a half. I woke first and then he did and we greeted each other with smiles and kisses until I realized what time it was and how angry and upset Granny could be. I couldn't call her because his phone was disconnected.

" 'I gotta go, get to a phone and go home,' I told him. I had forgotten to dry my clothes. He gave me one of his pullovers and a pair of his jeans, which were way too big, of course, but I rolled up the legs and tied a belt around the waist. I used the hair dryer on my sneakers and put on a pair of his sweat socks. I know I looked a sight, but I didn't care. I was actually happy I was wearing his clothes. I put mine into a paper bag and then he walked with me to the bus stop. We found a pay phone on the way, but vandals had stuffed gum into the slots.

" 'I'll just go home,' I told him. "You going to come to school tomorrow?' I asked.

" 'Yeah,' he said. 'I'll meet you at the locker in the morning.'

"The bus came moments after we arrived and I was on it, waving good-bye. He looked so happy and my heart was so full and hopeful. All the terrible things in my past seemed to dwindle next to his smile. Love is really more powerful than hate, I thought.

"I didn't know. I didn't know," I said and paused.

I was crying and my throat felt so tight, I couldn't swallow.

"Easy," Doctor Marlowe said. "You're doing really well, Star. It took a long time to get you to this place. Don't give up."

I nodded, took a deep breath and looked at the girls. They all wore looks of deep fear. Misty and Jade had actually moved closer to each other and Cat embraced herself so tightly, anyone would think she would come apart if she didn't.

"Of course, Granny was very upset when I got home. She had given Rodney dinner and cleaned up, but it was like her to leave a plate out for me and keep some of her stew warming.

" 'Where've you been, child?' she asked from her rocker. 'I've been sick with worry. How come you're dressed like that? Where's your clothes?'

" 'They're in this bag, Granny,' I said holding it up. 'I got caught in a rainstorm and soaked to the skin.'

" 'Whose clothes are these?' she asked, her eyes more like two tight slits of darkness.

" 'They're Steve's,' I said and then I tried to explain it all quickly. 'I'm sorry, Granny, but I had to rush out like that and I couldn't call you. Steve's father didn't pay their phone bill and their phone was disconnected. I knew something

154

was wrong with him when he didn't come to school today.'

"I told her about Steve's bruise and I told her I had spent time with him to help him. No," I added quickly, anticipating Jade's question, "I didn't tell her what we did or too much detail.

" 'That don't sound good, Star. You best not go to that house no more. You promise me that,' Granny demanded.

"I shook my head.

" 'I can't promise you that, Granny. I love Steve,' I said.

"She made a face, twisting her mouth like strips of clay and folding her brow like folding a fan and shook her head.

" 'Lord, you can't be in love with no boy that fast and you're too young for such talk. Now don't go making the same mistakes your momma made and end up on the same dead-end road, child. You promise me you won't go to that house no more, hear?'

"I shook my head. 'No,' I cried back at her. 'I'll never make such a promise.'

"I ran to my room and just stood there staring at myself in the mirror. Then I started to cry. She came to my door.

" 'You eat anything?' she asked.

" 'No.'

" 'Well come on then. Have some of the stew.'

" 'I'm not hungry,' I said.

" 'You don't eat something hot after getting soaked, you're going to get sick. Have some stew,' she insisted. 'Get out of those clothes and come on out here now, Star.'

"I didn't want to aggravate her anymore so I did what she wanted. Rodney sat at the table while I ate and told me about a new game he played in physical education class. I only heard bits and pieces. My thoughts kept returning to Steve and our time and the way he looked when I waved to him from the bus. It was like a picture that had been printed forever and ever on my brain.

"Granny didn't talk any more about it. She went into the living room to watch her television shows. Rodney sat at her side and I went to my room and just thought about Steve, fantasizing about our lives together, how when he was old enough to get his trust, we would go off and get married and love each other better than any two people. I'd be a good mother and he would be a good father because we both knew what it meant to have terrible parents.

"Before I went to sleep that night, Granny came to my doorway to ask if I was feeling okay.

" 'Yes,' I said. 'I'm sorry. I didn't mean to worry you, but I had to go,' I told her.

"She stared at me for a long moment and then said, 'I hope you're still a good girl, Star. The easiest thing to lose in this world is your own self-respect and that's the hardest thing to get back, too. Just look at your momma.'

"I didn't want to keep being compared to Momma. I hated the thought, so I just turned my back and pretended to go to sleep. I didn't for a long time. Granny's face and words haunted me even though I didn't feel like I should think of myself as being a bad girl. I really and truly loved Steve. I couldn't imagine loving anyone else more and I thought if this isn't love, if I'm too young to be in love, then I'll never be in love.

"Granny was fine the next morning. Rodney and I left for school. I was never so excited to go. I was at the lockers early and loitered, trying to act as if I had to straighten mine out. It grew later and later. The first bell for homeroom rang and Steve wasn't there again. I waited anyway and was late to homeroom. My teacher was upset and bawled me out, but I couldn't hear a word he was saying. I kept anticipating Steve's arrival.

"I can see in your faces that you know what I'm going to say next," I told the others. "He never came to school."

"Oh no," Misty said.

"Yes," I said. "He and his daddy got into it even worse than before. I don't know why. I never really found out details, but I always thought it was because of me."

"How come you never knew? Didn't Steve tell you?" Misty asked.

"He couldn't," Jade answered for me. Her eyes nearly stabbed me with their penetrating glare. "Right?"

"That's right," I said. "He couldn't."

"Why not?" Misty asked.

"His daddy beat him badly. He fought back

and his daddy hit him so hard, he knocked him into a coma."

With my eyes closed, I said it all as fast as I could. It was like swallowing cod liver oil or something. You wanted to get it over fast.

No one spoke or asked anything. They waited for me to open my eyes and take a breath. I looked at Doctor Marlowe. It was always hard to go past this point. Sometimes I could; sometimes I couldn't.

"That whole day in school, I kept hoping he would show up late. I knew he would if he could because he would anticipate what I was going through, but he didn't come. The day ended and he never appeared. I was like a zombie in class, hardly hearing anything. In math I didn't even hear the teacher call on me and I got bawled out for that, but I didn't much care.

"I was afraid to go to his house again right after school, afraid of what Granny would say and how angry she would be, but I didn't know what to do. I couldn't call. The phone was still disconnected.

"I told her Steve hadn't come to school. She lectured me about how it was between him and his father and I shouldn't get too deeply involved, but I was deeply involved. It was too late to think of not being there. I couldn't eat. I did the best I could to please her and I helped her with the dishes and then I moped about, hoping that somehow he would get to a phone and call me. Why doesn't he call? I kept wondering.

"I was tempted to run out again so many times that night, but I held onto the hope that he would be in school the next day and the mystery would be over. Maybe he was still just too embarrassed to show up with that bruise and egg-shaped swelling on his cheek.

"Of course, I couldn't get around the fact that he would have called me or gotten some message to me about it somehow. Something was wrong. I knew it in my heart. I felt it in my stomach.

"The next day I waited at the locker and he didn't show up, but instead of going to homeroom, I went to the office and asked to speak to the guidance counselor, Mr. VanVleet, who had once given Steve advice about his father, advice he respected.

" 'What can I do for you, Star?' he asked. 'You're going to be late for homeroom again, you know.'

" 'I know, but I've got to talk to you,' I said desperately enough for him to agree. He told his secretary to inform my homeroom teacher I was with him.

" 'Okay,' he said taking his seat behind his desk. 'What's so important this morning?'

" 'I'm worried about Steve Gilmore,' I said and I told him how we had planned to meet at the lockers yesterday and then how I waited today. I told him quickly why I was worried. He didn't interrupt, but when I was finished, he looked down at his desk and then shook his head and looked up at me.

" 'I'm sorry to tell you that there was domestic violence in that house night before last. The police arrested Steve's father after some woman made a nine-one-one call and the paramedics found Steve unconscious. He's in St. Mary's hospital and he's in a coma,' he told me.

"Things get kind of gray for me at this point," I said. I looked at Doctor Marlowe.

"I guess this is about where we are, where we've been," I said, looking at her. She nodded.

"I can remember the pain. It was like when you get a paper cut and it stings so bad, only this cut was right through my heart. I felt all the blood leaking out. My head was suddenly very light and my legs felt wobbly, but I didn't faint. I remember that I nodded and left the office.

"When I stepped into the hallway, I remember I looked down toward my homeroom, but I found myself outside the school. I ran a lot. Eventually, I got on the right bus. Don't ask me how I knew where I was going at that point. I guess something takes over inside you, some second-self that works you like a robot.

"The next thing I remember I was standing in front of the hospital. I didn't think at all about being in trouble for running out of the school or about what it was going to do to Granny. I guess what I thought was if I could just speak to Steve, maybe hold his hand, he would be all right again and our future together could still happen.

"That's what gave me the strength to go into the hospital and ask for him at the information desk. They said he was in something called intensive care and only immediate family could visit. I said that was fine. I was his sister. No one challenged me so I followed directions and went to the elevator.

"When I opened the door to intensive care, I was greeted immediately by a nurse. Once again, I said I was Steve's sister. She looked like she didn't believe me, but something in my eyes must have told her that if she didn't show me to him, I would be trouble.

" 'He's still not responding,' was all she would say. She brought me to his bed and told me I could stay about ten minutes.

"His head was bandaged and there was another big bruise on his face, just on the left side of his jaw. His eyes were closed so tight the lids looked glued shut. They had all sorts of stuff flowing into his arm.

"I worked my fingers around his anyway and I began to talk to him.

" 'I'm here, Steve,' I said. 'It's me, Star. I knew something was wrong when you didn't show up. I knew you wouldn't let me down. Please get better, Steve. Please,' I pleaded.

"They said I was crying very hard and that was why the nurse came over and made me leave. The way it worked was I could return in an hour, actually every hour on the hour for ten minutes or so. Some nurses let me stay longer than others. I talked to him more the second and third times. One time I just held his hand.

"No one else came to see him of course. His daddy was still in jail and probably wouldn't have come. Debbie certainly wouldn't come.

"I didn't eat any lunch and I never thought about Rodney until it was too late. I found out later that he waited for me and then gave up and found his way to Granny's all right. He was crying when he arrived and Granny went frantic and called the police. By then the school had called anyway and I guess Mr. VanVleet came up with the thought that I had gone to the hospital to see about Steve.

"Late in the afternoon, before the police came to the hospital to look for me, something happened in Steve's head. Some kind of a blood clot. I don't know all the fancy medical details but his heart stopped and they went into an emergency procedure just as I walked in again. I saw them all around his bed working on him. No one seemed to notice I was standing there. I saw and heard them give up.

"I only have very sketchy memories after that: a policeman talking to me, walking toward the front entrance of the hospital, running, being in the street, being in some alley someplace, wandering through a lot full of garbage and broken-down cars, some old man smiling at me, his mouth toothless, grimy hair on his face and chin, standing by a heavily-traveled street and then . . ."

I looked at Doctor Marlowe.

"Then they said I tried to kill myself by

walking out on the street and just standing in the way of traffic. Car horns were blaring all around me, people were shouting, one car hit its brakes too fast and another crashed into the rear of it. Glass was shattering. There was so much noise, I put my hands over my ears and pressed them so hard, they actually carried me off the street and put me into the back of the police car with my hands still pushing on my head.

"I ended up in a hospital, too. Suddenly, I blinked and found myself looking up at a strange doctor who smiled at me and told me to try to stay calm. I went in and out of sleep. Granny told me I was there nearly two days before I was alert enough to know where I was and who she was.

"Naturally, I was very frightened. Later, I found out about all the trouble I had caused, especially the car accidents. Someone had gotten hurt. Granny was so upset, I was afraid she would have another heart attack, but I felt so weak and tired, I just slept a lot.

"They put me in psychological therapy in the hospital and then I was released and Granny had to bring me to court where a judge put me on some kind of probation connected with seeing Doctor Marlowe.

"That's how I got here. Remember, we were kind of answering that question?"

The others all nodded simultaneously as if their heads were somehow connected by wires.

I sat back.

"Just recently, I found out where Steve is

163

buried, but I haven't been able to go to the grave. Granny isn't too happy about the idea. She's afraid it might cause me to do something stupid like step out on a busy highway again. Doctor Marlowe is supposed to help me deal with all that, right, Doctor Marlowe?" I asked, not hiding my fury.

"I'll try my best, but you have to be the one who ultimately helps yourself, Star. You all have to make that commitment, to want to do it," she said.

"That's convenient," Jade said. "If we get cured, you're a hero. If we don't, it's our fault for not caring enough about ourselves."

"Would you rather I pretended to have all the answers and some miracle in my back pocket?" Doctor Marlowe asked her. Jade just stared. "I would have thought all of you were tired of hearing false promises."

"What am I supposed to do, forget what happened?" I fired back.

"We all thought Jade was saying something stupid at lunch when she wished we all had Alzheimer's disease like your mother," Misty said. "Maybe that wasn't so stupid. Maybe all this is stupid."

"I hate my memories," Cat suddenly added. "I don't want you to make me remember them," she said to Doctor Marlowe with more anger and aggression than any of us had seen in her so far.

For a moment I felt like we were all ganging up on Doctor Marlowe. If she felt it, she didn't mind it. She looked like she almost welcomed it.

"You're all going to do this," she said slowly, "look for people to resent, targets for your anger. Your anger's justifiable, understandable, but if you let it run your lives, it will ruin them. What I want is for all of you to first admit to your anger, deal with what's caused it, and then use it, make it work for you. In short, free you from it."

"Right," Jade said and looked away.

"Did you want to tell us any more today, Star?" Doctor Marlowe asked.

"I don't think so," I said.

"What about your mother?" Misty asked, suddenly remembering her.

"Oh yes, Momma. She called while I was in therapy at the hospital. She was in North Carolina and now she was with Aaron's cousin instead of Aaron. Granny told her what had happened and she was disgusted and told Granny that she couldn't handle a problem like me just yet. She had intended to send for me and Rodney, if you can believe that, but once she heard about the trouble, she thought it would be better if we stayed where we were until she was better established.

"What were you saying about promises, Doctor Marlowe?"

"Exactly, Star. You know which to take seriously and which not to at least," she said.

"That's not hard, Doctor Marlowe. Any promises my Momma makes I throw in the garbage. Anybody else, I just don't believe."

Misty laughed.

Cat nodded and Jade looked up at the ceiling, took a deep breath and announced she was sufficiently depressed for the day.

"I hope you'll get more from this than that," Doctor Marlowe said.

Jade looked at me.

"I did," she admitted. "I'm sorry. I didn't mean to belittle your story."

"I'm not worried about it," I said.

"I know you're not," Jade fired back.

We stared at each other for a moment and then Doctor Marlowe stood up and we all followed her out.

"All right, girls. Thank you again. Jade, tomorrow?"

"I wouldn't want to miss it for anything," Jade said dryly. "The chance to be another Star."

She looked at me and laughed and I laughed too. Sometimes, it just felt better to laugh.

We stepped out.

Misty's mother had a cab for her this time.

"Daddy's got another bill to pay," she announced.

Jade's limousine was right behind it. Across from it Cat's mother waited and watched us like some bird, not looking directly, but nevertheless we could see she was aware of every step we took.

Granny pulled up last.

"What's your grandmother's name?" Jade asked. "You've only referred to her as Granny."

"Betty," I said. "Betty Anthony."

Jade sauntered over to the car as she walked toward her limousine.

"Hello, Mrs. Anthony," she said. "I'm Jade."

Granny smiled and said hello.

"Hi," Misty said hurrying toward the taxicab. "I'm Misty."

"Hi," Granny called back with a laugh.

Cat moved slowly toward her mother's car and paused to nod at Granny.

"I'm Cathy," she said but lowered her head and moved quickly away before Granny could respond.

I got into the car.

"That girl's plenty shy," she said referring to Cathy.

"Yes," I said. We watched her mother pull away first. She looked upset.

"Well," Granny said. "They seem like nice girls for spoiled rich girls."

"They're not all spoiled. Well, maybe they are. I don't know," I said. "Maybe it's not bad to be spoiled," I muttered.

"You all right, child?"

"Yes, Granny."

I looked back as we drove out. What a funny caravan we made, I thought.

"So you did fine?" Granny asked.

"I don't know, Granny. I did what Doctor Marlowe wanted me to do."

"Well, that's good, isn't it, child?"

"I don't know," I insisted.

Granny looked disappointed. I was tired of

disappointing her.

"Yes," I said. "It's very good. Granny?"

"What is it, Star?"

"Tomorrow, after breakfast, would you take me to the cemetery where Steve is buried?"

She looked at me, her eyes filling quickly with fear.

"It'll be all right, Granny. I promise. I just want to say good-bye, Granny. I never said good-bye. And it's time."

Granny nodded.

"Okay," she said. "If you think it's time, then it's time."

"Thank you, Granny. Granny?"

"Yes, child."

"I love you."

She smiled.

"And I love you, child."

It can't all be bad then, I thought.

Can it?